A Kripslod In The Realm

Volume One
of
The Kripslod's Tale

D. J. Kenny

A Kripslod in the Realm.
Volume One of The Kripslod's Tale
Copyright © 2012 by D. J. Kenny

All rights reserved. No part of this book may be used or reproduced in any manner whatsoever without written permission except in the case of brief quotations embodied in critical articles and reviews. For information contact: kripslod@gmail.com

This is a work of fiction. Names, characters, places and incidents are either products of the author's imagination or are used fictitiously. Any resemblance to actual events or locales or persons, living or dead, is entirely coïncidental. But don't worry, Mr Kenny is now getting the help he needs.

4 AE

Printed in the United States of America

ISBN 978-1482080117

A Word of Caution!

This is the first part of a multi-volume story, so you won't find out that it was the butler who killed Sire Periwinkle, by poisoning his vindaloo with iodates, until volume three.

A Note About Punctuation:

This book is based on a much more extensive original extraterrestrial text written in the Realmspeak language.

It has been translated into English by a team of highly qualified, but vastly underpaid professionals. What our team lacked was a skilled grammarian, so we have had to handle that task ourselves.

As someone undoubtedly wrote, "There is nothing as inefficient as a committee writing a sentence." Perhaps not, but a committee punctuating a sentence must be a close second. Each of us on the team has taken a try at a chapter or two—and it shows. As we produced this volume on a very tight budget, we hope you, our patient and understanding reader, will let us slide this one time. If you have trouble, try imagining you're reading this on an Internet blog, or that it is a piece of experimental literature written by a far more talented and creative person who's thinking outside the box.

Translators' Acknowledgments:

We would like to thank the individuals responsible for keeping our office so neat and tidy. They never realized that so much of their time would be taken up by our after-hours chatting and our repeated requests for their enlightened and enthusiastic opinion on various points in this book.

We would also like to thank Matt and Laura—the young couple who own the print shop down the street. They have been most courteous, generous, and obliging.

Thank you all, most sincerely!

—The English Translators

Introduction to the Third and Forth Editions

It has been brought to our attention that many readers are having trouble with the content of the first six chapters of this book. Many have reported that they gave up reading the book after failing to see any indication of an actual story.

In the original extra-terrestrial Realmspeak text this book was translated from, the first few chapters were used to introduce characters and events that will have a barring on the rest of the story and we felt that it would be best if we followed that same pattern in our translation. We could not have been more wrong. Introducing characters does little good if the reader never reads further.

To correct this problem we now will include this brief outline of the story so that our readers will have a better understanding of what will follow:

Our story takes place during our present time—the last decade of the twentieth century through the first decade of the twenty-first century on our American calendar.

The location is in and around our Galaxy's great super power, *The Thenardite Brokered Federation of Planetary Republics and Political Bodies*—a.k.a. 'the Realm.'

At the present time, the Realm consists of many planetary States with a variety of different forms of governments under the central control of a powerful federal bureaucracy.

Among the Realm's more noteworthy resident species are: humans (descendants of specimens acquired thousands of years ago from Earth), the dinosaur-like halotrichites, the large egg-laying mammalian palagonites, the cat-like cerargyrites, the lemur-like lanarkites, the remarkably dog-like ettringites, and the shape-changing thenardites.

The Head of State and chief executive of the Realm is called the Imperial Majesty. At the time covered in this story, many inside and outside of the Realm have come to believe that, with the help of her all intrusive security services, the

Imperial Majesty has become a tyrant.

One of the Realm's member States (Ettring) is ruled by a hereditary monarch—King Leudoberct CXVII, who chaffs under federal control and desires to make his planetary State a totally free and independent country.

Bordering the Realm are several small independent nations and a few Realm protectorates.

Currently, the nation that gives the Realm the most trouble is *The Republic of the Clinohumite Free People.* This republic consists of a single planetary system bordering the Realm's Third Octant. It is inhabited by the descendants of human refuges from a long past genocidal war and exists in a constant state of hostility with the Realm. However, not being in a position to take on the Realm in conventional warfare it relies on piratical harassment and terrorism.

Now that we have set the scene for you, here is what you will find in the first six chapters of this book:

Chapter One will introduce you to the Realm-born human medical technician, Thresher Selverlinck.

Chapter Two gives you a look into the world of the Realm's troublesome neighbors—the Clinohumites.

Chapters Three and Four lets you meet Teodor Korzeniowski, a human from Earth who finds himself forcefully recruited to help the Clinohumites in their ongoing battle against the Realm.

Chapter Five introduces the king of a vassal nation who would shake-off the Realm's overlordship whatever the cost to the rest of Galactic civilization.

Finally, Chapter Six should help you to reason on whether the Realm is indeed the peaceful, united, and democratic paradise that the Realm Ministry of Culture and Tourism demands people believe it to be, or the repressive dictatorship that many of the peoples of our Galaxy have learned to fear.

—*The English Translators*

On the Races of Our Continuüm

"First, you should understand that we are all The One's children and that means we are all family.

"As one of my parents liked to say, "One, two, or three caudal orifices—it really doesn't matter, for it still gets all the work done."

"I like to say that we do not all look alike, but we all think alike."

—*The Great Siblinghood,* Tymorann Alphrontex

Table of Contents

☐	Introductions	3
☐	On the Races of Our Continuüm	6
☐	Table of Contents	7
☐	Figure One	8
One	Med Tech Thresher Selverlinck	9
Two	The Humans of Clinohum	15
Three	Teodor Korzeniowski	23
Four	Non-Complainers	31
Five	King Leudoberct CXVII	37
Six	Protector of the Realm	41
Seven	Liberation?	45
Eight	The Realm	53
Nine	And Then He Met Her!	59
☐	Figure Two	64
Ten	Above the Waters of Palagon	65
Eleven	Guard Admiral Reinier	77
Twelve	A Visit from Parent	81
Thirteen	Gin and Tonic	87
Fourteen	A Test of Loyalties	105
Fifteen	The Wolnyn System	111
Sixteen	Catalyst	113
Seventeen	Retirement Plans	129
Eighteen	*Admiral I Taisto Station*	135
☐	Figure Three	160
Nineteen	The *Cult of Adalheidis*	161
Twenty	The Privateers of Clinohum	165
Twenty-One	The IGSS *Eviscerator*	167
Twenty-Two	The Waiting is Over	173
Twenty-Three	Meanwhile, on *Palagon Station*	179
☐	Translators' Endnotes	187
☐	Previews of Coming Distractions	206

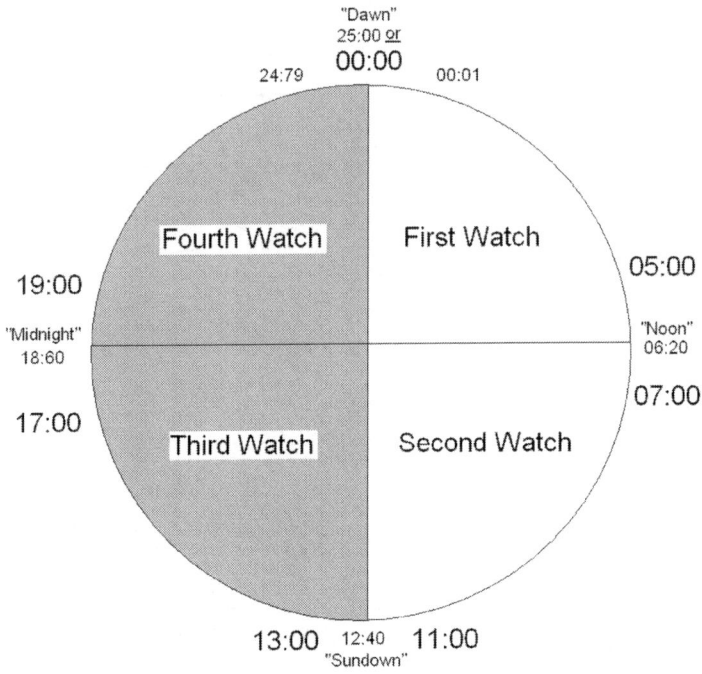

Fig. 1. Realmtime or "Planet Palagon Time."

We found that many of our readers were becoming confused when it came to understanding the time references mentioned in this book. So we hastily put together this diagram. This would be the standard clock used on stations and ships in the Realm. On Realm planets, other than Palagon itself, the hours would be expanded or condensed to coïncide with planetary time. We hope it helps. (See also, Endnote #15.)

Chapter One
Med Tech Thresher Selverlinck
1748 fTF [1992 CE]

Anatase Station, the Realm

The human med tech finished with her patient by giving her a few instructions, "Well, Citizen,[1] I think we're all finished here. Just be careful with it. And keep it covered. It will take a few more days to heal up completely. ... If you experience any significant discomfort, come back in and see us right away."

"Ew! But it looks so ugly. How long do you think it will take for my fur to grow back?" the young cerargyrite asked.

"That will take some time. In fact, with that degree of injury you may eventually need to see a specialist. Don't worry. Just give it a month or two and if the fur hasn't filled in completely, then by all means, contact us. We can put you in touch with someone who can help." Med Tech Thresher Selverlinck[2] explained.

They left the examination room and, as Thresher walked partway down the corridor along with her patient, she further instructed, "Just stop at the reception desk on your way out. And in the future, let's watch where we stick our tail."

As Thresher passed the day's break and meal schedule, she stopped to make certain that she was once again on First Lunch. Ever since her university days, Thresher had been in the habit of taking an early in the shift meal break. Here at Matteloet-Cotenghys Realmcare[3] Clinic, that was rarely a problem. Most of her fellow third-shift co-workers had far more exciting off-work lives than she had, so their circadian rhythms tended to be quite different from hers.

After a stop at the hygienic station, Thresher made her

way to the company break area. Of all the places Thresher had worked in her life, this one had by far the most pleasant and restful employee dining area. There were what looked to be windows on three sides of the room. They were probably [video] screens, but ether way, they presented a view out onto a lovely rainforest-like landscape. Today, a myriad of small, brightly colored, winged invertebrates were fluttering around the dimly lit forest floor. The view almost made up for the food.

The 'human specific' food in the dining area was about the worst Thresher had ever eaten, but it was provided at no charge, was said to be nutritionally balanced, and reported to be, 'certified human non-toxic,' so she choked it down most workdays rather than going out and wasting half her break time queued up at a local eatery.

On the room's fourth wall, just next to the doorway, was the food purveying equipment and a small area used to customize your meal. Over that hung a large and formal portrait of the Realm's Imperial Majesty[4] and a screen for viewing newscasts and entertainment videos.

Thresher acquired her lunch, gave the representation of her beloved Imperial Majesty a smile and, since no one else was present, set the screen to a scheduled newscast about the commissioning ceremony for the Realm's newest and most advanced warship. She took her seat opposite the screen. She hated to ignore the entertaining invertebrates cavorting outside, but she really wanted to watch this report.

The coverage of the commissioning ceremony had already started, {"... ship and place it at the disposal of our Realm, our Citizens, and our Imperial Majesty. I hereby instruct Fleet Realmwide Operations to record the Excarnator Class System Control Vessel,[5] hull number 27563n411740, to be henceforth assigned the official designation, SCV-700, TFSS[6] *Predator* and recorded as a strategic asset of Operations Third Octant. By order of the Legislature's and our Imperial

Majesty's representative, Fleet High Admiral Maximinus,[7] Chairperson—"}[8] Thresher's attention to the newscast was interrupted by a cerargyrite[9] female looking into the room.

"Thresher?"

"Piritta?"[10]

"It's me, Thresher! Oh, I'm so very glad I finally found you. I communicated with your dad a few days ago and he just couldn't remember the name of the place you were working at now. A former co-worker of yours, at a clinic down station from here, gave me this location."

"Had to be Launo, he's a dear. I'm glad you found me, Piritta! What brings you all the way out here to *Anatase*?"

"It wasn't *that* far. Torsti and I live back on Almandite-Five now. He had to come out here for business and I thought that if I came along I might just get a chance—"

{"... Fleet Captain Deodatus ..."} the screen said loudly.

"I'm sorry, Piritta. Let me adjust this volume lower. There. Now we can talk better. Can I get you something?"

"Do they have *rowprifth*?"[11]

"I should hope so. *Gliezial*?"

"A little, please. Thresher, I hope I'm not interrupting?"

"Not at all. I was just watching the commissioning ceremony for that new SCV. It's supposed to be the most powerful warship the Realm has ever built. Possibly, the most powerful warship in our whole Galaxy!—Sorry, I'm just like my dad. He keeps track of the Fleet the way most Citizens watch over the doings of their hometown meadowball team. He knows what ship has been reässigned where and which officer gets the highest scores on their fitness tests. That's what comes of spending forty-nine years in the Fleet. But I'd really rather catch things up with an old friend. I'm so sorry I missed your mating ceremony. I had just started working here.—Well, I just couldn't afford to miss work and travel over to Haughton. I'm very sorry, I really would have loved to have been there."

"I know, Thresher. I would have loved having you there, but I know how tough it is to get away just after starting a new job.

"At first, I was very upset at you when you declined my invitation. My mom set me straight. She told me that if I really wanted you there, I could always forgo a few luxuries at the ceremony and send you the funds instead. I guess I didn't miss you that much," Piritta confessed with a cerargyrite friendship smile.

"Well, we're still friends, and I'm very happy to see you again. You look great! Your fur is so shiny! Ether you started eating a lot of eggs or mated life certainly agrees with you."

"You seem to be doing just fine by remaining single. I mean that, Thresher. Just a few months ago, I had lunch with Frida and she told me that she had spent her last holiday staying with you. She told me she had a great time. Just like back in our carefree days at university. I love my mate very much, but sometimes I miss—what should I say? Our free spirited times as dormmates. Oh, and I should also say that your fur is very pretty. But it always was."

"Piritta, you always forget that you cerargyrites have fur and we humans have hair. How is Frida[12] doing at Guard Officers Training School? I haven't talked with her since she stayed with me. That has to be eight or nine months ago."

"Frida will always be Frida. I communicated with her just before Torsti and I left to come out here. She says she's studying so hard that she has little time for anything else. I think we both know that's not true. Although, I did get the sense that she might be settling down just a little bit. You know, studying more and partying less."

"I don't think the Guard Officers Training School is much of a place for dancing and singing."

"You'd be surprised. My uncle manages a first class hotel over on *Illite Station*. He likes to tell about the time they had this group of inebriated Citizens running up and down the corridors, laughing, singing, pounding on the other guest's doors, stuff like that. A few of the more temperate guests suggested my uncle call the Federal Police. Problem was, the drunks were with the Federal Police. They were having some type of convention."

"Piritta!"

"Thresher, I'm just repeating my uncle's story. He says it really happened. And at *his* hotel."

"More to the point, Frida is concentrating on her studies. Good for her! You know her problem at university was her high intelligence. It all just came so easy for her. That's why she had so much free time for festivities. But I think we all had our fair share of bad judgment and Frida wasn't anything like the worst among us. Remember the time Fuzzi Eck'crawd[13] went missing for three days?"

"You know, Fuzzi's mated now and has two hatchlings? Her oldest already started primary school. I don't know about you, Thresher, but I stopped getting older ten years ago. Trouble is all our friends keep reminding me that it isn't true. ... But on the subject of Frida and speaking of refusing to grow up: Our future officer in the Guard is still hopelessly infatuated with that ettringite prince of hers."

"She'll be all right, Piritta. Deep down she knows it will never happen. The future king of the ettringites can't mate with a mere commoner. Even if she is as good looking an ettringite female as our friend Frida."

"To bad she just doesn't bob her own ears and show up uninvited to a royal ball or something. Just take a chance and get it over with. I mean, he might take a fancy—"

"Like in a tale for hatchlings. Frida's smitten, but she's not a fool. She once told me that it is a *very* serious crime on Ettring to impersonate a cropper. Even in other parts of the Realm it is illegal for an ettringite to have their ears cropped without express permission of the king of the ettringites. In fact, even our Imperial Majesty can't reward an ettringite in that way. I thought that's one reason why Frida applied to the Guard and not the Fleet in the first place. She's not likely to meet Her Beloved, [Medical Officer Fleet Commander HRH Crown Prince Hroderich][14] serving in the Guard."

"I talked with her long enough to know she's far from over him. It's a shame, Thresher. I read he's a lot older than Frida, and his dad is getting very impatient with his lack of a mate. He won't be available too much longer."

"Poor Frida. Well, if it's any consolation to her, she can always come and live with me when we're both retired, old, cantankerous, and still unmated."

"Don't you worry, Thresher. If I can find a mate, I'm sure you and Frida can both find one too."

"Thank you, Piritta, but I'm really not looking for a mate anytime soon. I've got my career to consider first."

"Thresher, I know you'll need to get back to work soon, so what do you say to letting us meet you after work and taking you out for [a late] dinner. Our treat. That will give you a chance to meet my mate and prove to him that I wasn't always the quiet and demure type of female I fear I'm quickly turning into," Piritta said while getting up and placing her empty mug in the cleaning unit.

"That's fine with me. I'm afraid we'll bore the poor male with our university stories. — Well, that's just the price he has to pay for mating a fully paid-up member of the Sisterhood of Placer Twenty-Six. … Goodbye, Piritta, and thank you. I'll meet you out front around 18:60."[15]

After Piritta left, Thresher turned back to the screen and what was left of the commissioning ceremony. It was almost over and all assembled were now joining together in the Realmgreeting, {"Our Imperial Majesty!"}

"Our Imperial Majesty!" Thresher said out loud while giving a precise salute to the Imperial Majesty's portrait.

A few minutes later, Thresher disposed of her dishes, turned off the screen, and returned to work.

Chapter Two
The Humans of Clinohum
1749 fTF

National Security Center,
Planet Clinohum, Clinohumite Republic

"Sire[16] Formaybeel? Captain Diederik Wagherts is here as directed. May I show him in?"

"Please do. ... And, Lotte, please have my notes on *Operation Kindred Feeling* organized and ready for this afternoon's meeting with the Security Council. Thank you."

"They'll be ready, Sire.—Captain Wagherts, Sire Formaybeel will see you now."

"Good morning, Sire Formaybeel. I hope I'm not interrupting?"

"Captain Wagherts, it's never an interruption to see an old comrade-in-arms and our nation's favorite privateer. Please, come in and make yourself feel at home. There's [beer and wine] in the cool box. Help yourself and, please, call me Sjoerd."

"No *ag-brocht*,[17] Sjoerd? Not even for a favorite comrade or an old privateer?"

"I'm sorry. No! I'm not comfortable seeing humans drink the traditional beverage of our race's most hated enemy."

"Do you remember Professor Hubrecht Gherstecore?"

"From the Ministry of Antiquities. Yes, I remember him. A little ... (He finished by gesturing a twisting motion with his right hand.) Wasn't he with you and Jutte on the *Ranger*?"

"That's him. He introduced me to *ag-brocht*. The CO of that Realm ship—the one who just happened to come along in time to offer us assistance when we ran into that trouble out at Heureka—was an ettringite. The Professor used our chance meeting for an impromptu hands-on lesson in the ancient and—in his opinion—much maligned culture of the Black and Tans.[18] In my opinion they may be the lowest scum in the Galaxy, but they do make some first class liquor."

"But as you said, Captain, "Lowest scum in the Galaxy." I find it troubling when my fellow humans feel that it is acceptable to imitate those who in the past enslaved and murdered members of our species. As the poet said, "Racial loyalty is easy to develop and easy to forget.""

"A poet also said, "A poet's impromptu words, so wise when removed from the burden of context." Don't worry, Sjoerd. Remember, I'm from *Iconium*. I will never forget what the Black and Tans did to my family. I can drink the ettringite's liquor and still hate them with every cell."

"I'm sorry, Captain. Please forgive a forgetful old friend. If there is anyone in this faithless universe I can trust it is most certainly you. You and Senior Captain Jutte Renstaes that is. Risking your lives out among the stars while we in the Supreme Council must work tirelessly here at home. Our nation owes you both a great deal of thanks!"

"So very kind of you. I'll still drink your beer. Would you like my report from the Realm now, or did I risk my ship and my crew racing back here for socializing?"

"Again, I'm sorry, Captain. I seem to have upset you with my prejudice against humans drinking *ag-brocht*. Let's not sully our long friendship with meat flavored trivialities."

"And I'm sorry too, Sjoerd. With my executive laid up in sickbay, I'm just a little [on edge] right now."

"Nothing serious I hope?"

"Sometimes the crew of a target foolishly fights back. Lieutenant Peussyn took some light taking our last prize. It was iffy at first, but Doc says he'll be fine now. With a nice big scar to impress you planetsiders as an added bonus."

"You privateers are doing a lot of good work. We would be hard pressed to keep our nation strategically supplied without the equipment and raw materials you acquire. And to be honest, being able to disavow your actions helps diplomatically as well. We need allies amongst our neighbors. And we need to keep the Realm agitated, but not too agitated."

"Speaking of agitated, Sjoerd, I'm sure it will warm your spleen to learn that our friendly neighbors in the Realm are presently experiencing a bit of political turmoil. My contacts tell me that a few long time members of the Realm's legislative body have been finding creätive ways of supplementing their meager State-provided salary. They also tell me that their Imperial Majesty is not very happy about it. It looks like there is going to be a purge and it could include some high ranking members of their military as well."

"Is it actual impropriety or just an excuse to clean out the heretics? Since we got wind of that new battleship of theirs, we have been waiting for something like this to happen. It could be the house cleaning the Imperial Majesty needs to remove any impediment to an all out attack against us."

"The trouble with your well thought out opinion, Sjoerd, is that the ones most likely to disappear before the onslaught of the Imperial Majesty's wrath are the ones most vocally against us. Several of the suspected miscreants are ettringites. A few are even croppers. If it was a prelude to an attack against our nation, I would have thought that most of the purge would be directed at our fellow humans, or, at least, against those of the other races who, through long inoculation, have grown tolerant of us. My contacts in the Realm didn't find any human legislators or even human military officials on the Political Police's list of suspects."

"That doesn't make any sense! Are you certain your contacts can be trusted?"

"Who told you about the battleship *Predator*? And who is now telling you about all the trouble in the Realm?"

"Maybe we were wrong about the Realm's human

population. Maybe they are more subjected and powerless then we long thought them to be."

"Sjoerd, I'm sorry to light-up your ideas again, but you know you should spend a little time in the Realm. Remember when I went on that extended mission to Acm? I learned a lot. And I realize that was seventeen years ago, but things can't have changed that quickly. The humans of *The Thenardite Brokered Federation of Planetary Republics and Political Bodies*[19] are far from being a subject people. Back then, the highest court in the Realm had two or three human senior Judges. Their secret police[20] had a few human officers, and their navy [21] had far more. And something more up to date—I just found out that the executive officer of that new battleship you're all so worked up about [TFSS *Predator*] is a human. His name is Ector Ventsoen. Born and raised on Acm, and as I understand, the grandson of a prominent local politician."

"Captain Wagherts, I am seriously troubled by our fellow human's readiness to support the Imperial Majesty of that accursed Realm!"

"What I find most troubling, Sjoerd, is how much the humans and ettringites in the Realm seem to be willing to cloak their prejudices towards one another. It's like the Realm's humans just choose to forget the last three thousand years of our race's history. I think that could be our greatest danger. The humans of the Realm don't seem to care, one way or the other, what their government does to us. They must think their fellow Citizens—the ettringites—are more kin to them than we are!"

"Perhaps in the near future we can change their minds, Captain. Please get yourself another drink. And then, I should let you give me your report. I have a meeting later with our President and the Security Council. Updated reconnaissance from you will be valuable to our discussion."

* * *[22]

Chamber of the Security Council, Planet Clinohum, Clinohumite Republic

The adjutant opened the door and stepping into the room announced to those present, "Dames and sires of the Security Council! Be upstanding for our Nation's President!"

Sire Staas Ollevyere, the president of the Supreme Council of *The Republic of the Clinohumite Free People*[23] entered and, after exchanging greetings, took his seat at the head of the main conference table.

"Captain Clayszuene, please secure the door on your way out. *No one* is to be admitted until this meeting is over. And no one is permitted to stay in the outer office either."

"Yes, sire. You will have a completely secured perimeter. Please, let me know if you find you need anything. I will be at the security desk at the end of the corridor. Number twenty-seven. ... Sire President!"

The president waited until the screen indicated that he would not be overheard by anyone outside of the room; then he addressed his fellow attendees, "Sires and dames, thank you all for coming to this security briefing. As you already know, our neighbors in the Realm have finished testing out their newest battlewagon. Unfortunately, that will mean they will soon have two very formidable military groups in close proximity to our border. If there was ever a good time to be a Clinohumite—this is certainly not it. We need to consider the very real likelihood that we will be attacked and possibly very soon. Sire Formaybeel has looked over a proposal put together by the military. And as this is a democracy, and as all of us have been elected by our fellow citizens to represent their interests, their hopes, and unfortunately their fears, he would like your thoughts on the matter. Sire Formaybeel, if you would please give us your presentation."

"Thank you, Sire President. We call it, *Operation Kindred Feeling*—the recruitment of between eighteen hundred and two thousand Earth-born humans to come to Clinohum and help us defend ourselves against the militaristic intentions of the Realm and its dictatorial leader.

"I know what you all are thinking, "What can a few thousand volunteers from the Motherworld do against the greatest threat to peace our Galaxy has ever seen?" Honestly, from a fighting standpoint, nothing at all. If all the able-bodied humans of Earth were to come to our aid, we would still be hopelessly outnumbered by ten thousand, perhaps twenty thousand to one.

"As I've said, in a combat situation they can not help us. However, psychologically they can do a great deal for our cause. Imagine what a boost to morale it would be to see our Earth-born brothers and sisters leave their safe and peaceful planet and be willing to put themselves in harm's way in order to help protect our free human way of life. That would certainly be the stirring that our own complacent and excessively comfortable young people need to inspire them to patriotic zeal! Who knows but that this show of racial single-mindedness might not even bring our fellow humans dwelling behind our enemy's borders over to our side. Despite what you may have heard, the humans of the Realm are not powerless. They, like our own children, are comfortable with the status quo. They fear they will lose too much if they side with us, but they are not powerless. As we speak, many human officers sit in command of patrol boats, destroyers, and other warships of the Realm's Fleet.

"Interesting? Not the half of it! My office has it on very good authority that the executive officer of the Fleet's newest battleship, the TFSS *Predator*, is a human. If we can convince the Realm's human population to think of themselves as humans first, ... well, that tyrant, that mocker of the Gods, the Realm's twice cursed Imperial Majesty, might have more to think about than her current bad neighbor policies.

"When this operation is authorized, my department will

proceed with Step One: The infiltration of Earth society. I have suggested that Captain Hinchelyn take the lead in that initial phase of our—"

Dame Lieke Wielancke, chairperson of the Agricultural Committee, heatedly interrupted, "Of all the foolishness! We are just going to travel over to the Earth and drag thousands of savages away from their families and their tribal fires. Then bring them here to Clinohum and expect them to willingly fight for us? Are you insane! We don't have enemies enough already—now you have to import them!"

With her remark the containment fields of social convention were de-energized. For the next hour or so, it was [bedlam] in the conference room, with each person present vying to make their own opinions and concerns heard—usually with rudeness and very loud voices.

"Criminal waste of time!"

"We just expect the Fleet of the Realm to let us travel through their space on the way out and back from Earth?"

"And just what will our primitive earthlings do against spaceships? Hold their breath and throw rocks?"

"Madness!"

"Insanity!"

"With our mining stations still so ... so criminally unprotected, we waste our time on this nonsense!"

"We need more warships, not spear throwing savages!"

"But it doesn't really cost us anything to try." Sire Gerolt Satelaeres finally said, cutting through with reality.

"Sire Satelaeres, you have our attention."

"Thank you, Sire President. While you and all my other learned colleagues were otherwise occupied in discussing the merits of Sire Formaybeel's proposal, I was carefully examining his documentation. In my humble opinion, if it can be carried out discreetly—and by that I mean without causing concern to the Earth human population or calling attention to ourselves by either the Realm or the government of Earth—then we have only to concern ourselves with the cost of such an operation.

"As I understand it, we will need to send about one hundred thirty operatives to Earth. These operatives will need to be well versed in the Earth human language—*la langue française*" he said reading from Formaybeel's notes and then continued, "And additionally will need to unobtrusively dwell on Earth for a period of about two years. They will select our volunteers and then five transport ships will need to travel a round trip through the Realm's territory without alerting our enemies. Once on Clinohum, the Earth natives will need to be cared for and educated before they can be utilized for our propaganda purposes.

"That's all there is to it. It will work or it will fail, but either way, it costs us very little in manpower, funding, or equipment. Also, we should not forget about the cost in time. While this operation is undergoing completion, we can utilize the majority of our resources in giving Dame Admiral Keilliaert those ships she keeps earnestly requesting.

"One of my constituents has plans for producing as many as fifty commercial cargo ships. With financial aid from our national government these hulls could be, on very short notice, converted to quite adequate warships for our national defense. Perhaps we should consider it."

In the end, the matter was settled. Sire Satelaeres' influential constitute would get the money he needed to lay the keels of his flotilla of extremely expensive merchant vessels. Dame Admiral Femka Keilliaert would get a promise of available ships to quickly arm in case of an emergency. Sire Formaybeel would have permission to send to Earth for moral support—with Captain Tygo Hinchelyn handling recruitment, Admiral Junsteman seeing to transport, and Senior Captain Jutte Renstaes in charge of housing and training the new Earth-born recruits when they finally arrived on Clinohum.

Chapter Three
Teodor Korzeniowski
1751 fTF [1997 CE]

Planet Earth, Solar System

At 6:10 PM, on the tenth of October, 1960 CE [1719 fTF,] the Korzeniowski[24] family of Utica, New York, were blessed with a new member. To Konrad, Murielle, and Nicholas was added a new little child—Teodor. He was named after a famous Polish cavalry officer and patriot of the nineteenth century, but there were scarcely any similarities between him and his namesake. Our Teodor was afraid of horses and grew up to be thought of as more a narcissistic and nihilistic cynic than any form of patriot. As for the likelihood of his being appointed an officer in any branch of anyone's military? In short, not a chance.

His home life was typical of his era. Not quite early 1960's American TV family, but close.

The Korzeniowski family lived in a modest ranch style home in a suburban neighborhood.

Mother Murielle was the homemaker and was active in school affairs.

Father Konrad was the breadwinner and worked long hours at the office and even longer hours at home keeping their yard immaculate.

Brother Nicholas was the typical big brother, five years older and far more outgoing and athletic then Teodor, but they still managed to get along reasonably well with one another. Nicholas had many friends, and they usually spent their time playing ball and talking about cars. Teodor had far fewer friends and spent his time watching TV and reading comic books.

Each summer, the whole Korzeniowski family, including a

cousin or two, would spend a few weeks camping and fishing up near Blue Mountain Lake in the Adirondacks. These summer trips were the only times Teodor would see his father without a tie or his mother in canvas shoes.

Teodor enjoyed these times in the mountains very much. Although, he was never really that pleased to be with his more physically inclined and bulling cousins or that thrilled with sitting in a dark and chilly boat early in the morning fishing with his dad. What he did enjoy, was going off by himself looking for rocks and crawly stuff while pretending he was a scientist exploring a newly discovered and possibly dangerous planet.

Teodor was far from scholarly, but he did moderately well in school. Without doubt his best subjects were: geography, history, science, and foreign languages. To his preschool English, Polish, and Canadian French, he added middle school Spanish, high school Latin, and later college German and Russian. Certainly, his worst subjects were: art, shop, mathematics, and anything that involved organized sweating. In just about the middle range of his scholastic aptitudes one would find the study of English and American literature. He loved to read, but he never could understand just how he was supposed to interpret what he read. For example, "What did Melville really mean when he said the sky was blue?" Questions like that would endlessly puzzle and trouble him.

He obediently read every book he was told to and then spent hours at the local public library refining his own tastes. He liked classic adventure stories, mysteries, and fantasy, but it was science fiction that he loved best. Teodor saw it, read it, and talked about it every chance he got. When he was a child walking home from school, he would imagine he was the captain giving orders on the bridge of a starship. When he was older and had a day off from work, he would rent a video player and half a dozen science fiction movies, then disappear to the basement to spend the day anywhere but on mundane planet Earth.

Before he found it financially necessary to move closer to the big city and spend his life in a fabric covered box (he would never stop telling people that his *home* was Utica,) he would regularly stop over at his parent's house and help out by cutting the grass with their old, and rather dull, manual push mower. At those times, he would again be lost to the real world and would find himself on the bridge of a spaceship ordering, "More power to the engines!" Only to have his chief engineer reply, "That's all she's got, Captain!"

He studied geology in collage but never got any jobs related to that subject after he graduated. The jobs he did get were just that, jobs. They paid the bills, but they were dull and predictable. He tried to make the best of it, but now after years of adulthood, he more and more wished he could somehow be taken away from boring old Earth and spend his life in the furthermost reaches of our Galaxy.

The boredom and predictability of his job and his life began to splinter apart on Thursday, July 24, 1997. The day when a tropical storm came to Manhattan, NY.

Teodor loved weather like this, but only when he could safely and comfortably watch it through a window and with a coffee and a doughnut next to him on his desk. He had been at this job for two years now, and that made him more or less senior enough to have the privilege of a window.

The rain and wind was starting to pick up in intensity and Teodor could see water collecting down below him in the parking lot. The forecast was for the remnants of the tropical storm to slowly work its way up the coast for the rest of the day and throughout the night. Someone had said that up to ten centimeters was expected to fall in Central Park before it all worked out of the area on Friday afternoon. He didn't mind. He wasn't going anywhere, but back and forth between work and his crummy apartment, for the next few days anyway.

The electronic mail handling software on his workstation brought him out of the daydream he had been quickly slipping into. It was a communiqué from the Boss-On-The-Floor-Above. It was a company-wide note of parental concern forwarded from Corporate, "Due to the worsening weather conditions on the northeast coast of the United States of America ... Employees in the effected area are cautioned to avoid unnecessary travel and to drive carefully." A helpful list of good driving practices for inclement weather was attached.

Having dutifully read the warmly personal and timely advice, Teodor returned to his daydream. A second piece of electronic mail arrived and then a third. Teodor once more returned to twentieth century Earth and read them. One was an offer of improving his personal life by enhancing certain physical attributes of his wreck of a cubical entombed body. He directed that one to the bit bucket. The last was another message from the Boss-On-The-Floor-Above.

"CRAP!" Teodor said out loud.

It was another one of those great ideas his bosses would come up with from time to time, "To: Teodor Korzeniowski. Re: Inter-divisional Cross Training For Maximizing Fiscal Security and Survivability." The gist of the letter was: Tomorrow (Friday) he would need to be here in the office for meetings at 10:00 and again at 1:15, but on Saturday morning at 11:45, Teodor was to meet someone named Axelrod in the parking lot of the company's division in Jamestown, NY, so that he could acquire the necessary paraphernalia that would permit him to have access to the building at 8:00 AM on Monday morning (July 28, 1997.) Afterwards, he would take over the assignments and responsibilities of a certain co-worker who would be fulfilling a reciprocal assignment here. This arraignment would be in effect until next Thursday (July 31, 1997.)

Teodor was to be back here to work next Friday. The letter ended with a supposedly happy note: "Feel free to come in at noon on that Friday!"

Teodor quickly worked out what he thought was the best of several bad eight hour drives to Jamestown. He now found it impossible to return to his daydream, so he began researching the company's travel reïmbursement[25] policy and making the necessary lodging arrangements.

Later, when he got back to his apartment, he started right in on packing for his trip. There wouldn't be any chance of stopping home and seeing his parents, and he doubted he would do any sightseeing, so he thought he would only need his work clothes. But he did make certain to pack a good selection of his favorite paperbacks to get him through the motel room nights. And for the long ride, several new science fiction stories read out on cassette tape that he recently purchased for just such a contingency.

The next day, he packed up his old car and for an expensive and frustrating change of pace, drove to work rather than taking public transportation.

At 2:00, Teodor found out that his 1:15 meeting had been re-scheduled for Tuesday and that it wasn't really important that he attend anyway.

At 2:50, he retrieved his car and started out to Jamestown.

Four hours later, he entered the outskirts of Binghamton. Teodor was listening to a great story on his tape player and was beginning to think that at least the driving part of this trip wasn't going to be that bad after all. Of course the work would be as boring and predictable as always, but the trips out and back would give him a chance to enjoy a few tapes.

A former longtime resident of Binghamton—a man who was responsible for so many of the amazing stories Teodor enjoyed on late night TV re-runs—might have had something very witty to say if he could have known what would happen to Teodor when he finally stopped for dinner eighty miles or so further down NY route 17.[26]

At about 8:30 PM, Teodor entered Big Flats and found a roadside place that called itself a family restaurant, so he decided he'd take a chance and finally stop for dinner. He had a lot of stuff on his front seat, but since there were no other cars parked in front of the building he had no trouble finding a parking spot he thought he could keep an eye on from inside while he was eating.

He stood for a moment just inside the door and gave the place a quick look around. It seemed clean enough. With the exception of three men sitting in a booth near the entrance, he seemed to be the only other customer. "Of course. It was probably a little late for the dinner crowd. After all, this wasn't the big city." he reasoned to himself.

The two men sitting facing Teodor took notice of him for just a moment and then, without any acknowledgment, joined their companion in looking out the window towards the road, and what was troubling to Teodor, also at his car.

The waitress came out with dessert for the men and told Teodor to find himself a booth. A moment or two later, she brought him a menu and saw to his place settings.

After browsing the menu for a while, he finally settled on southern fried steak "w/white gravy," fries, and despite the late hour, coffee. (Years later, Teodor would tell those around him that he had been a rather strict vegetarian at least since his high school biology days, but that, like so many of his statements, needs to be [taken with a grain of salt.])

As he ate his meal, he occupied himself by listening in on his fellow diner's conversation. One of the men spoke heavily accented English and good *Québec* French. He was the one who communicated with the waitress, and most of the time she eventually understood. Teodor almost helped out the one time she didn't, but then he thought that it might not be a good idea to get involved. Anyway, it wasn't that important a comment the *Québécois* was trying to get across.

What the native language of the other two was, Teodor hadn't a clue, since they only seemed to speak in very poor store-bought 'Radio French.' The gist of their conversation seemed to consist of: the two trying to keep the one unconcerned about their present difficulties and enthusiastic about achieving their long term goals. It appeared that they had needed to travel to a new location and to hastily meet up with some associates after an unfortunate border crossing incident that they may not have needed to have gotten involved with in the first place; and something or other about what just happened to their car due to the fact that one of them was a very, very, bad driver. The *Québécois* kept pointing out that it would have been far better for all concerned, if they had left the piloting of automobiles to him and the piloting of *"vaisseaux spatiaux"* to them. They got a little heated for a moment or two, and then one of them went off to use the pay-phone. When he returned, the conversation turned to an appreciation of Teodor's old clunker out in the parking lot. About that time, a police car pulled in and the officer came in for coffee and a little sports talk with the cook.

The *Québécois* gestured to the waitress, and she brought the men's check over. At that point, Teodor found their conversation took a rather hurried, sinister, but somewhat comical turn. It went something like this,

"Here. I'm sorry, I forget which one is their currency?"

"That one. But not a hundred! I can't give her a hundred for this. I thought we were supposed to be inconspicuous. ... There! I'll take that. You two wait outside while I pay."

"I'm so glad you decided to work for us."

"*With* you! Now please, just nonchalantly walk outside, and admire your stars while I finish up. And keep those weapons out of sight"

Teodor thought he should get the police officer's attention, but just as he started to, the officer's radio interrupted.

A moment or two later, the police officer rushed out onto the road traveling west at high speed and the three men hurried off eastward across the parking lot on foot.

Teodor suddenly realized just how tired he was and how out of practice he was in French, so he thought it might be just as well he hadn't started anything. He finished up his meal with what he remembered was his father's all-time favorite "traveling-time" dessert—Boston cream pie.

It was about 9:30, when he left the restaurant and got into his car. It was an old clunker now, but when new, it was rather pricey and so it had many of the latest and greatest features. An indicator light on the dash informed him that one of his doors was not properly fastened. The fact that someone had used a 'Clinohum Heavy Industries Model 96-11-h compact ultrasonic cutting tool' to severely damage the door latch on the passenger-side rear door might have had something to do with that.

Teodor turned around to look into the back seat and found one of his French speaking friends looking back at him. He was gesturing with some sort of devise in his hand, and after Teodor complied by unlocking the other doors, the other two joined him in the car.

One tried to sit on the seat next to Teodor, but was seriously inconvenienced by the litter of empty soda cans, candy, chips, uncomfortably hard and sharp plastic cassette cases, and other assorted stuff. Teodor thoughtfully picked out and stowed the tapes and cases and then brushed the junk onto the floor. When his last passenger was finally seated, a discussion commenced as to whether Teodor was the only one present that could successfully drive a manual transmission. He was and so he did.

On July 26, 1997 CE, at 3:38 AM EDT, his wish was finally granted, and a then unconscious, but undoubtedly happy, Teodor Korzeniowski left Earth on a faster-than-light transport ship bound for the the planet Clinohum.[27]

Chapter Four
Non-Complainers[28]
1752 fTF [1997 CE]

A clandestine military installation, Clinohum Republic, Alabanda System

"Senior Captain Renstaes. You wanted to see me, ma'am?"

"Yes I did, Lieutenant Schoonemacker. Come in and close the hatch behind you. ... Recently—"

"Good morning, ma'am."

"Oh, good morning, Mr. Schoonemacker. Are you done?"

"Yes, ma'am."

"Very good. ... Now, as I was saying, recently, I noticed that one of your students isn't using a translator any longer."

"Yes, ma'am. That would be the American Teodor Korzeniowski. He's getting very good with our language. Hardly any noticeable accent."

"Let's be very careful, Mister Schoonemacker. We don't want to lose sight of our mission. Right now, If they're going to be of use to us as propaganda weapons, they can't be too much like us. They have to remain foreign and exotic. Also, we don't want them learning more about us than they need to know. There will be plenty of time for them to discover all our faults and idiosyncrasies later. Do we understand each other, Mister Schoonemacker?"

"Yes, ma'am. Will you be joining the class today?"

"I certainly will. I think it's time to tell them a few more horror stories about our *friendly* neighbors in the Realm. I'll stop by around 06:40 hours to give them a lecture and a little after class studying to do. ... That's all, Mr. Schoonemacker."

"Very good, Senior Captain. I'll let them know to expect you."

* * *

Teodor Korzeniowski sat taking notes as Schoonemacker, once again, lectured them fervently about all things Realm. Teodor thought Lieutenant Schoonemacker was [OK], just a little too earnest and repetitious when it came to teaching his class about the evil, sinister, and oppressive dictatorship, overshadowing his beloved, nonbelligerent, and peace-loving, little country. Teodor had to be quick and concise as he tried to keep up with his teacher:

- Humans originally collected from Earth by ettringite explorers working for the Palagonite Empire.
- Shown around the Palagonite Empire as curiosities.
- As numbers increased they were used for slave labor.
- For no reason, ettringites started killing all humans.
- Most races in the Empire ignored the killings at first.
- Small numbers of the other races did try to help humans.
- Finally, after many atrocities, all the races got involved.
- Civil war started.
- Palagonite Empire collapsed.
- Thenardites took over and forced other races to submit.
- Called their new country, *'The Thenardite Brokered Federation of Planetary Republics and Political Bodies.'*
- Also called, 'the Realm.'
- Supposed to be a democracy, but still ruled by Palagonite Imperial Majesty under secret control of thenardites.
- Planetary States of the Realm kept in line by the Fleet.
- Citizens of the Realm kept in line by the Guard.
- Technology about the same as Clinohumite's.
- Realm has greater number of ships, but over larger area.
- Most Realm military commanders obey rules of war.
- But ettringites are never to be trusted. Ever!
- All ettringites hate humans and want to harm them.
- The Realm is secretly run by the thenardites.
- Thenardites are very, very dangerous!
- They can change into the body of those they eat.
- Never come into direct contact with a thenardite!

Teodor's note taking got a lot easier when Schoonemacker slowed down the hectic pace of his lecture and began showing them pictures of his subjects on the screens:
- Ettringites look like Dobermans standing on two legs!
- Thenardites also look like dogs, but unlike ettringites, they walk on all fours. Look like a striped, yellow-brown dog with a stiff (kangaroo-like?) tail.
- Palagonites look like a big, very hairy, and carnivorous theropod dinosaur.
- Lanarkites look like Earth lemurs.
- Cerargyrites look like a two legged Earth cheetah.

* * *

After the [slide show], they stopped for lunch. Today, Senior Captain Jutte Renstaes was coming to give them a pep talk, so they had to stay in and eat their lunches in the classroom.

After he finished his lunch, Teodor started thinking about the things he had learned over the past few months and jotted down a little prose he thought captured the mood of his Clinohumite hosts:

"But the humans of the planet Clinohum are a very bitter people. As the old empire lay dying, their ancestors fled into the nearly impenetrable asteroid field surrounding the then uninhabited planet Clinohum. There they hid, there they waited, and there they relived over and over again, every hardship and deprivation; every injustice, slight, prejudice, and persecution that our species had experienced from the founding of the universe. They soon discovered that nothing tastes as good as well aged hate, frozen and re-heated generation after generation.

"When they finally came out of hiding and asserted their dominance over the planet Clinohum, they did so without the blessing of their neighbors in the

Realm, and they could not have cared any less. To them, the Realm was just a beneficiary of their old Imperial adversary. They had 'single-handedly' destroyed that enemy, and they would not rest until the Realm gasped its last breath as well.

"Never mind it was civil war that had destroyed the Empire of the Palagonites. Never mind that it was primarily the ettringites that had tried to exterminate the humans. Never mind that many palagonites and lanarkites had actively tried to render the humans aid. Never mind that thousands of cerargyrites had died fighting to protect human lives. Never mind the truth, lies slide down easier. No, let the inhabitants of Ilva write songs in lavish praise of their friends scattered about the planets. Let those of Phenak prance about holding the hands of species that would sooner eat them as pet them. Let the sentimental fools of Acm build memorials to their honored saviors. To Blazes with all of them! The humans of Clinohum would grow strong by engorging themselves on bitterness and hate."

Schoonemacker walked by and stopping behind Teodor read the dissertation over his shoulder. Finishing it, Schoonemacker came up abreast with his cynical American student. Leaning over and pointing to the document he made these three observations:

First, how was it that Teodor had ever been chosen to come to Clinohum in the first place?

Second, that Teodor should keep in mind that anger and bitterness did not preclude one's being in the right.

And third, that it would be best for both of them if Teodor never let Senior Captain Renstaes see what he just wrote.

* * *

Non-Complainers

After class, Teodor returned to the quarters he shared with the two Jamaicans. They were out doing something athletic so Teodor thought this would be a good time to catch up on his homework. He didn't get too far before his thoughts turned to Senior Captain Jutte Renstaes. Teodor had only seen her a few times but thought about her a great deal. She seemed to be very self-assured but a little young to be a commodore, or what the Clinohumites called a senior captain. "Maybe, they don't have a chance to get much older with this war going on?" he thought. She was very beautiful, but something in her face showed she had lived a hard life.

What troubled Teodor about her was her bitterness. It showed through in everything she talked about. It gave Teodor the sick feeling that he and his fellow earthlings weren't going to be asked to attack enemy starships, but marketplaces and public transportation instead. He wanted to warn her that they had bitterness like that on Earth too, and that it attacked civilization like a malignant cancer, but he thought better of it. That would probably be a very bad idea. You can't reason well with entrenched hate.

Teodor started thinking about the ettringites, the thenardites, and the Realm in general, "Those ettringites are amazing, they look just like Doberman pinschers. How is that even possible? What evolutionary need would ever lead to a dog-like animal into developing a bipedal walk and primate-like hands? Even if the creätionists are right, why would a god make something that looks like a human wearing a really realistic dog costume? ... Or could they have been put together thousands of years ago by some advanced civilization? Maybe, they were the results some genetic experiment that went terribly wrong.

"And what about those thenardites? They are supposed to be these shape changing monstrosities. ... They just look like a dog that any young human child would want to run right up to and pet.

"A dog-like, tawny furred animal, with strips only halfway up its back, and a ridiculously stiff tail. What on Earth do they remind me of?

"And another thing, if the Realm is so powerful and ruthless, why have they never attacked Earth? Who would stop them? The Clinohumites? Not while their entire survival strategy seems to consist of hiding behind their heavily armed asteroid belts."

What about his hosts? "If this militaristic superpower wants to destroy them so badly, what stops them? Is there another superpower in the Galaxy? Even if there is, you can always find an excuse for the invasion of a weak and insignificant little nation. Can any space-faring civilization ever be as bad as the Realm is said to be?

"Then, there is the hardest question of all, can the Clinohumites be trusted? Just what is their angle?"

Teodor went back to his studies, but again, only for a moment. Then he started thinking, "You fool! This is what you have always dreamed about. We're needed. These humans need us. Hell, the whole human race needs us! This is the real thing. Spaceships, anti-matter torpedoes, lasers. It's what we've dreamed of all our life! Don't screw it up with any more cynical crap doodled in a notebook.

"Tomorrow, we get our uniforms and then soon, we're to be shown off to the whole Clinohumite Republic as a much needed boost to their morale. Imagine, me a boost to morale. And I'll be helping to protect the Earth! Helping Mom and Dad, ... and Nicholas and his family too!

"But what if Schoonemacker, Jutte, and the others aren't telling the whole truth? What then?"

Chapter Five
King Leudoberct CXXVII
1753 fTF

The Royal Apartments, Audamar Palace, Planet Ettring, the Realm

The Provider of the Royal Meat quietly opened the door to His Highness, the King of the Ettringite's[29] private chamber and whispered, "Holy Father? Holy Father, are you awake?"

"What is it, Raimund?"

"Holy Father, Her Royal Highness, Princess Hilditrut, begs your patience and requests an audience. Does, My Lord and Holy Father, permit her to enter?"

"Of coarse, Raimund. My sister's oldest child is always welcome. Send her in immediately!"

"Yes, My Lord and Holy Father."

Raimund turned to find the princess right behind him and not at the Location of Respect where she should have waited. Flustered, he attempted to relate to her the King's answer, "Your Royal Highness, Princess Hilditrut. His Most Exalted and Beloved—"

She pushed past him and introduced herself, "Hello, Uncle Leudoberct. I hope I'm not interrupting your afternoon nap."

"It is never an interruption, Hildi.—Excuse me for a moment.—Raimund! You may leave our presence and shut the door securely behind you.

"Yes, My Lord and Holy Father."

"It is a pleasure as always to meet with you, Hildi."

"Thank you, Uncle. Mother sends her love." the princess answered, and after exchanging the customary racial greetings,[30] used the interface to verify they could talk without being overheard.

"Return mine to her. Now, I hardly think it was for the purpose of delivering greetings of familial love that brought you here today. Is this about Eburwin's retirement?"

"It is, Uncle. General Eburwin's health is not good and he is certain to ask for your permission to retire and enjoy his fading years pursuing less strenuous activities."

"He was always a loyal and hardworking commander of my bodyguard. I will miss him and his loyal discretion. He has been privy to so many delicate matters of State. ... Still, he has worn himself out in my service and deserves a rest. I mean that, Hildi. I think we can let him see out a few more years of life, undisturbed."

"You have always been the model of gratitude, Uncle. The High Priest of Adalheidis[31] would like you to consider his mate's brother Herbert as a replacement."

"And you, my child, are the model of self-control. You brought me that request without [laughing]. I think Colonel Vilmar will be my choice as a replacement for ever loyal and trustworthy General Eburwin."

"The Priesthood feels that Colonel Vilmar is not a true fearer of the Gods."

"And what does my loyal and loving niece think?"

"Colonel Vilmar has no fear, no love, no loyalty, and no beliefs, that are not those of His Highness and Holy Father, the King of the Ettringites."

"Excellent! I could expect no less from the future commander of my bodyguard."

"And what of the High Priest of Adalheidis?"

"What of him? Does he present another petition?"

"High Priest Ecgric would request that you give him your permission and your blessing to use his influence over the Taciturnians and their *Cult of Adalheidis*[32] to arrange the assassination of the Imperial Majesty of the Realm."

"That would solve nothing. Her [familiars], the thenardites, have very carefully arraigned an efficient constitutional procedure for replacing her. I do not think we could have any reason to expect a better relationship with any of her more likely successors."

"Ecgric plans to arrange it so that the blame would fall on the Clinohumites and possibly even on the human population of the Realm as well. He hopes to bring about their eventual extinction"

"I have never found humans to be so vile that I cannot tolerate sharing my Galaxy with them. At least not any more vile than any other foreign race."

"I agree, Uncle. I have known quite a few members of that race. And I have found them both useful and aesthetically acceptable—when they mind their place. Unfortunately, Ecgric has informed his followers that the Goddess Adalheidis does not share our tolerant attitude. She wishes the human race destroyed completely and with expedience."

"It is my belief that when a Deity has a concern they are certainly capable enough to carry out their own wishes without requiring mortal involvement. The Taciturnians are becoming a problem. Ecgric is also becoming a problem. For that matter, so are the Priesthood in general. What is a kind, benevolent, and grateful, monarch to do?"

"If the Taciturnians are clandestinely, (most clandestinely,) allowed to carry out Ecgric's racist plans and they should regrettably be discovered—"

"That would be the end of them. How sad! They were such loyal servants of the Gods. Should we concern ourselves about any unpleasant consequences?"

"I think not, Uncle. If the Imperial Majesty is regrettably harmed in any way, we might expect a close inspection of our planetary government by the security services of the Realm. However, if certain documents should come to light ... let's say, showing that it was your very own bodyguard that discovered and thereafter reported on the criminals. It certainly would not be your fault if the Imperial

Majesty's own security services failed to protect her."

"Is there any real possibility of their plan succeeding?"

"Perhaps, Uncle. They plan to steal an Xz-7 mining torpedo. I believe you and your mate, our beloved Queen, were made aware of their considerable destructive power a short time ago."

"We had a most informative briefing and demonstration, courtesy of our friends at the Realm Department of Strategic Materials. They also provided a rather tasty lunch afterward, if I remember correctly."

"Well, Uncle, the Taciturnians plan to steal an Xz-7 from RealmRock, and then detonate it near the Imperial Majesty's shuttle when she visits the TFSS *Excarnator* after it's finished with refits in a few short years. They believe they will soon have infiltrated all the necessary agencies and Realm departments to bring their plan to a successful conclusion."

"What do we know about Guard Admiral Reinier?"

"Despite repeated tries by his most devote mother, Reinier still regards the Taciturnians to be a superstitious pack of disloyal and dangerous fools. He is, most regrettably, loyal first to the Realm and second to our illustrious race."

"I wonder where his loyalty to me places? Never mind. Let us give quiet support to High Priest Ecgric's plans, but we will be certain to make adequate preparations to give our most precious of all Citizens, the ever diligent Guard Admiral Reinier, help in flushing out these noisome terrorists as well. Hopefully, we will be able to render him aid at a time that is just right for *all* concerned.

"Be certain to give Ecgric the unequivocal understanding that, despite the Guard Admiral's divided loyalties, Reinier is still very valuable to our person. It wouldn't do for the Taciturnians to take any action against the commanding officer of the Realm's Political Police. At least, not until our own plans for him have come to fruition."

Chapter Six
The Protector of the Realm
1753 fTF

HRH Prince Gnaeus Memorial Station
Proculus System, the Realm

For Teuvo, the worst part of being an officer assigned to Fleet Intelligence was having to work under a Citizen like Fleet Vice Admiral Crin.[33] The second worse part was not being able to tell his loyal and loving mate about the worst part. Everything about his job was of the highest secrecy and the last few days were no exception.

Tonight, Teuvo arrived home in a bad mood. Not being able to tell Minttu that it had nothing to do with her, and everything to do with the Fleet vice admiral, just made his mood worse.

Five days ago, a dispatch from the Office of the Imperial Majesty had arrived requesting a planing and feasibility study for an outlandish idea of sending a Fleet special operations unit to a moon in Clinohumite controlled space and rescuing a thousand or so Earth-born humans and then returning with them to the Realm.

At first glance it seemed a reckless risk of lives, but it was a request from the Office of the Imperial Majesty, so Teuvo got right to work on it. After a few days, he was confident the plan—to be code named, 'Audacity'[34]—was not only possible but also almost risk free.

Today, Fleet Vice Admiral Crin made one of his infrequent visitations to his *own* department and, looking over the study that Teuvo had worked so hard on, proclaimed it: "A stupid waste of time." The Fleet vice admiral then informed the Office of the Imperial Majesty of his unshakably uninformed opinion. "End of story! End of discussion!"

Tomorrow, he would find some real work for Teuvo to do!

Having dinner with his mate and the children put Teuvo in a slightly better mood. And later, while the children were finishing their homework and Minttu was watching the news reports, he took a nap in his chair. Sometime during the report on the usually mundane doings of the Realm's Legislature, he woke up and joined his mate in ever growing wonder at what was transpiring before them on the screen.

{"... Recent corruption scandal has left the House of the Planets bereft of some prominent members. Besides those directly touched by accusations of impropriety, there are also many that have found the whole business too wearisome to the mind and to the body. Today, we learned that Sir Merten, esteemed representative from Ettring and long time Speaker of the House of the Planets, has resigned, ... he has left with his family on a extended Realm provided period of rest. ..."}

{"... We can only imagine what additional changes to the prominent constellations of this august body will be made as the Political Police's investigation continues. ..."}

{"... Reporter at the House of the Planets has just informed us that all spectators have been removed from the chamber by the Federal Police. She has no word as to the reason ..."}

{"... Returning now to the unprecedented activities at the House of the Planets, [...] We have just been informed, by a senior member of the Federal Police, that only a few news service personnel will be allowed to stay. All other visitors must leave in order to allow room for the members of the House of the Citizenry to attend a special emergency meeting of both houses of the Legislature. ..."}

{"... They're filing in now and taking whatever seats they can find. It is certainly getting crowded in here. ..."}

{"... Our Imperial Majesty has just requested permission from acting Speaker of the House of the Planets Aelianus to enter the chamber and make her request to ..."}

* * *

{"... That was truly an emotionally charged address given by our beloved Imperial Majesty. [...] As we understand it, due to the current unprecedented threats to both our Realm's security and to its representative form of government, our Imperial Majesty has formally asked the Legislature and the Judiciary to approve of her appointment of current Guard Grand Admiral Karen to the exceptional[35] position of High Admiral of the United Forces. ..."}

{"... We have been informed by the spokesperson of the College of Law at the Second University of Palagon that only six times before, in the nearly Eighteen hundred year history of the Realm, has this position, sometimes called the Protector of the Realm, been created ..."}

{"... Of course the most famous Protector of the Realm was High Admiral I Taisto from back in the days of the Empire of the Palagonites. You may remember that it was High Admiral I Taisto who helped end civil war and brought about the peace that made the founding of our Realm ..."}

{"... This will undoubtedly be a lengthy process involving a significant amount of political give and take. ... If the Guard grand admiral is approved it will be the only thenardite to ever hold the position of Protector of the ..."}

{"... Of course, with several prominent opponents of [Imperial] involvement in the Legislative branch's constitutional responsibilities now under arrest ... "}

{"... Speaker of the House of the Planets Aelianus has just recognized the third motion to forgo debate, and will begin a vote of approval immediately. ..."}

{"... We may soon know whether we will have a High Admiral of the United Forces, a Commander in Chief of all the Realm's military and security services, a Protector of the Realm, to oversee both the external and the internal threats to our Realm, our Imperial Majesty, and our Citizenry. ..."}

* * *

By the time they heard the finale summation of the day's events, it was very late and both Teuvo and Minttu were exhausted.

Teuvo's rest would still have to wait, for just as he was getting ready for sleep, his superior communicated in, "Fleet Captain Teuvo. This is Fleet Vice Admiral Crin. Our Imperial Majesty!"

"Our Imperial Majesty! Is something wrong, Fleet Vice Admiral?"

"Teuvo, get the *Audacity* files together and meet me in my office at 18:00 hours. We need to shuttle down to Palagon and report to the Protector of the Realm, High Admiral Karen."

"Yes, sir. I understand, sir."

"Our Imperial Majesty! Fleet Vice Admiral Crin—out."

"Our Imperial Majesty!" Teuvo replied to the now blank screen, and then looking over at his long suffering mate, told her she would once again have to sleep alone. He had only seventy minutes to get back to headquarters, put his files in order, and then meet his superior as directed.

Teuvo knew a few officers in the Guard, but he had never met Karen. As he hurried out to meet the Protector of the Realm, he thought to himself, "What a way to make a first impression on the newly appointed highest officer in the Realm! No sleep, Ill-prepared, and with that *kripslod* Fleet Vice Admiral Crin in charge of the delegation!"

Chapter Seven
Liberation?
1754 fTF [1999 CE]

A clandestine military installation, Clinohum Republic, Alabanda System

Teodor was sitting alone in his quarters. His Jamaican roommates were off again, improving their bodies as he tried to improve his mood. The more Schoonemacker and the other Clinohumite instructors drummed in the horrors of the Realm, the more he wanted to [look behind the curtain.]

The danger from the Realm didn't seem to be all in his instructor's imaginations, though. Teodor thought about that conversation he'd overheard just the day before. Schoonemacker was talking with someone in the cafeteria and hadn't noticed that Teodor was sitting just behind them. The other man asked Schoonemacker if he knew why Senior Captain Renstaes "was so unreceptive?" That question was what caught Teodor's attention. Schoonemacker spoke very respectfully of his attractive superior and he explained her aloofness as being a result of her being a survivor of *Iconium*. That seemed to be more than adequate explanation for the other man and the subject was dropped.

This was not the first time Teodor had heard the name and he understood that *Iconium Station* (now called *Phoenix Iconium Station*)[36] was a mining center in the outer reaches of the asteroid belt [β.] He found the name interesting. It was one of only a very few names or words that he recognized as being from an Earth human language. He had added the name to a list of questions he intended to ask Schoonemacker about—if ever he could just sit down and talk privately with him.

Today, Teodor inadvertently learned more about *Iconium*

and that had led to his troubled thoughts this evening.

But first, Teodor made the discovery that he was not — never had been — actually on the planet Clinohum. No, he and his fellow earthlings were actually sequestered on a moon (Breithaupt-Seven)[37] orbiting a gas giant just inward from the asteroid belt[α.][38] His hosts had gone to a lot of trouble to make it look like they were on the surface of a sunlit planet. Apparently, in the interest of propaganda, they were keeping the lid on the earthlings until they were thoroughly conditioned to play the part of a brigade of Earth soldiers that had eagerly volunteered to come over and help their fellow humans on Clinohum fight against the murderous intentions of the Realm.

A short time after making that startling discovery, and while still snooping about in a part of the complex he had no business being in, Teodor overheard more about the tragic history of *Iconium Station*.[39]

Teodor exited though a hatchway that he thought would lead him into another mechanical race. To his horror he found that it actually opened onto a *very* well traveled corridor in the base's crew area. He tried his hardest to look like any other nondescript Clinohumite [worker bee,] and followed a couple who were obviously just off duty and heading for a food and drink area of some sort. It turned out that their destination was a tavern filled with military personnel and [AWOL] Teodor just walked right in.

He stood over in a corner and waited until he could walk out again without drawing attention to himself. He was wearing a haphazard assortment of his Earth clothing, his student uniform, and the military uniform he had recently received, and he was satisfied that his clothing wouldn't draw any undo attention to himself. It did look (to Teodor) that most in the room were either wearing a full uniform or a casual combination not unlike his.

He stood near a poorly lit table, as he waited for it to look

Liberation? 47

like—'It's just that his friends had stood him up'—and leave to find them. The table was occupied by two well lubricated soldiers arguing over old times.

"That's when we pulled out and ran."

"Afraid of a little Realm cruiser, were we? You know they never see us. You just never could keep your cover and wait them out. 'Keep quiet, keep still, and keep your head,' that's all there is to it."

"In yours, Dault! You weren't there. I was! And I knew that damn cruiser saw us ... and so I ran. I admit it. I ran. But I kept my head. No running back to *Iconium Station* with some damn ettringite's nose stuck to the back of my neck."

"Always with *Iconium*, Gortsen! Just because you survived a massacre all those years ago doesn't make you an expert on the damn Realm and its Fleet! For your information, the twice damn Black and Tans never smell humans."

"They could smell you a [parsec] away."

"That's not what I mean, Gortsen! Ettringites won't defile themselves by sniffing a mere human. It's beneath—"

"Don't tell me about ettringites! I know more about them than any human ever should have to know. A blazing lot more than you know! Fourteen bloody hours on *Iconium Station* and I got to know those monsters pretty damn well! Real up close I got to know them. Not like you [sissy] ship boys. Tell the computer and the target gets lighted. Do you even know how to fight it up with just a hand blade? Fourteen hours—fourteen hours and it was just me, Rygaert, Dyherrn, (maybe a few others) keeping those six little children alive. That's all. Out of what ... over nine hundred people? Blazes, I hate ettringites!"

Teodor looked down at the empty beverage containers lying about on the men's table and took a chance, "Excuse me, Gortsen, but wasn't Jutte one of those children?"

"You mean, Senior Captain Jutte Renstaes? Yes, she was one and Captain Diederik Wagherts. That politician from

Londinium—Dame Odelie—or something like that, she was another one. ... And who the blazes are you?"

Teodor reached over, and picking up an empty, put it up to his lips while stating with conviction, "Here's to the damn ettringites! May they choke on their own vomit!" With that he turned and, still carrying the empty, left the room.

Back out in the corridor, Teodor set the empty out of the way and started making his way back to the hatch that would get him back inside that mechanical race he had used to leave the classroom area. A few minutes later, he found what he was sure was the right hatch. He'd had sense enough to make a little mark on it earlier. Trouble was, now it appeared to be locked and he couldn't open it. Just as he was desperately trying to get it open, he was interrupted by unwanted company. He tried again to look like any frustrated maintenance worker, but this time, he got caught.

"Mister Peussyn! What do you make of our friend here?"

The younger of the two men unfastened his sidearm and then answered, "Never seen an outfit like that one, Captain. Looks like he made it from a charity drive for destitute navy veterans. I wonder where he's from?"

Teodor didn't like the look of the weapon or the man holding it, so he wisely told the truth, "Good day, Gentlemen. I'm just over from planet Earth. Name's Teodor Korzeniowski." and he slowly raised his hands in a way he hoped the Clinohumites understood meant surrender.

The captain responded, "So, you're one of Jutte's earthers. Does she know you're out wandering around?"

Teodor and his fellow expatriates must have been marked in some way, for all Mister Peussyn did was walk over a few meters or so, and activating an interface on the wall, received conformation. He gave his captain an all-clear gesture by securing his sidearm.

"What did you say your name was, my earther friend?" the captain asked with an insincere smile.

"Teodor Korzeniowski, Captain ... sir."

"I'm Captain Diederik Wagherts. Perhaps Jutte told you earthers about me? I'm the universally famous and staggeringly handsome privateer. This is my less-famous, but no less handsome, executive officer, Hendrik Peussyn."

"A pleasure." Lieutenant Peussyn said without any smile.

"Thank you, it is an honor to meet you both." Teodor said while smiling broadly and trying to sound *very* sincere.

"All right, Mister Peussyn. Let's help our Earth friend Teodor find his way back to class."

As the privateers firmly escorted Teodor back to the training area, Captain Wagherts did actually try to keep a little pleasant conversation going, "Well, Teodor, what induced you to get all dirty crawling about in maintenance races? Curious as to how our waste handling systems work, or are you just a frustrated spelunker?"

"I guess I was just wanted to sneak out and meet *real* fighters. I was getting a little tired of hearing about combat from just teachers."

Teodor quickly picked up on the fact that Captain Wagherts didn't like what he said, so he hastily added, "But now I know better about Senior Captain Renstaes. I just didn't have the whole story before."

Wagherts gave him the slightest shove against the bulkhead and, holding him there, sternly suggested, "Don't be a *kripslod*, [40] Teodor. I think it is a stupid idea to bring you troglodytes here in the first place, but if Senior Captain Renstaes thinks she can make something worthwhile out of you—then I'll back her up all the way. We've been through blazes together. Do you have any idea what it was like on *Iconium*? Lot of fun, but only for the ettringites. Nine hundred twenty-seven *human* civilians died on that accursed station! Jutte and I saw the damn whole thing. So just shut your mouth and do what your told, and maybe you can do something worth your keep and not just get others killed! If the ettringites ever make it to Earth, you had better hope they still need slaves to clean the parasites out of their fur!"

Hendrik gently touched his superior's sleeve, "Captain?"

"It's all right, Mister Peussyn. ... And I'm sorry, Teodor. I know you all volunteered to help us."

"Do you know the worst of it? *Iconium* was our own damn fault. After nearly a thousand years of just making faces at each other from over the fence, some of my fellow illustrious pirates went and hit an insignificant little freighter out near Digenite. It wasn't worth the energy it took to waylay it! But it was crewed by ettringites and I guess our fellow humans got a little too excited. When the crew of a Fleet warship finally found the wreckage they took exception to the way our fellow pirates had left the corpses of their fellow Citizens. The Fleet warship traced the pirates back home and the damn *kripslods* hid themselves near, of all places, a civilian mining station. You know the rest.

"I guess I can't blame the ettringites for wanting revenge. It's just that they missed those responsible and massacred innocent miners and their children instead. Maybe Professor Gherstecore was right. Maybe none of us has the wisdom to chart our course without his merciful God's navigation."

"All right, Teodor. Again I'm sorry. Let's just get you back."

Teodor didn't get into too much trouble. In fact, Lieutenant Raf Schoonemacker seemed to be happy with Teodor's show of initiative, but still, order and discipline had to be maintained. Tonight, Teodor would sit in his quarters while his classmates recreated.

Teodor sat on the end of his bunk, thinking about his discoveries and wondering why he still found it hard to fully trust the Clinohumites. Suddenly, he felt the world shake. A moment later, an earsplitting klaxon began sounding and the door to the corridor was dogged by invisible hands. There was a hissing sound from near the door, the room went quiet, and the room lights went out and were replaced with the stark glare of emergency lighting. Then, more shaking and the muffled sounds of thunder. Teodor considered changing into his military uniform, but a new and uncharacteristic thought held him back. If someone, or more likely *something*, found his dead body in the wreckage — well, he would like for them to know he was from Earth.

He took his school notebook and a few other things he thought might be valuable and stuffed them into the pockets of his jacket. He thought of his family back in Utica and almost cried from homesickness. What stopped him was the sight and sound of a small [squid-like] robot cutting through the door into his quarters. It was a robot, but it wasn't metallic like the ones in movies. No, this one was painted in an ever-changing camouflage finish. All Teodor could focus on was the wicked looking blades that the mechanical monster seemed to possess on the end of all of its tentacles.

The robot took what looked to be a can of spray paint and threw it into the room. There was a blinding flash accompanied by very high pitched thunder and Teodor instantly felt his heart stop and start — like the time lightning hit a tree just a few yards from the tent he was standing next to on one of his family's camping trips. Teodor fell down onto the deck and just lay there paralyzed by ten thousand spasms needling though his spine. All he could think of was that robotic [squid] serving him up like [sushi,] and if he could have breathed he would have screamed for help.

After a few minutes, his nervous system quieted down and he could breath again, but he thought it best to just lie there on his back and imitate a freighted opossum. He was just debating whether he should draw his tongue in, or leave it hanging out, when he saw movement near his head and nearly screamed for his mother. It wasn't the [squid.] It was a pair of human looking booted legs.

A human dressed in some sort of color-changing, all-encompassing, body armor knelt down beside him and put something, that looked all the world like a stud finder, on his chest. There was another human similarly dressed standing near and holding some sort of weapon aimed again at Teodor's much appreciated chest.

Teodor felt convinced that if the two gentlebeings didn't find a secure place to fasten a curtain rod, well then, it would be curtains for him.

The kneeling human told his companion that isotopic analysis showed Teodor was from Earth, took out a tool, and painfully stapled a tag to Teodor's ear. The standing human told Teodor to be quiet, stay in the room, and not under any circumstances try to remove his tag.

When the two soldiers left the room, Teodor got up off the floor and sat once again on the end of his bunk.

After thirty minutes, a young woman, way off in the distance, screamed for help in Spanish and Teodor started for the door. He was stopped just outside by a human in the strangest costume yet. This one was military looking, but was covered with bright yellow versions of the same letter from the Clinohumite's alphabet. It was the letter that represented the 'Ch' sound and Teodor correctly guessed it stood for, *Chasmird*, the Clinohumite word for a person trained in medical sciences. The Spanish woman stopped screaming and so Teodor coöperated with the med tech's demand that he accompany him to another location.

Teodor was escorted into a very large room with several transport ships resting in it. As he and dozens of other earthlings were herded into one of the ships, he looked over at a well guarded crowd of people and recognized them as many of his Clinohumite hosts. He saw a dejected, blood splattered, and very pale man sitting against a box of some sort with one of those medical people treating him. Their eyes met and as Teodor was just disappearing into the ship, Lieutenant Schoonemacker gave him a smile and a very earthling-like gesture of thumbs up.

Chapter Eight
The Realm
1754 fTF [1999 CE]

Realmcustoms and immigration facility, Sthene System, the Realm

In 1992 CE, back when he was still living in Utica, Teodor had purchased a light weight, black, cotton jacket with side pockets that closed securely by means of hidden zippers. He often wore this jacket when he traveled. It gave him a convenient and safe place to keep motel room keys, subway tokens, extra rolls of film, candy, unusual sea shells, fossil brachiopods and other indispensable and valuable objects.

The Friday afternoon he left for Jamestown was warm in Manhattan and hot in Binghamton, but by the time he met the one Canadian and the two Clinohumites in that restaurant in Big Flats, it was getting a little cooler and so he had followed his normal custom and was once again wearing it.

Teodor was still wearing it, when, a few hours later, he and hundreds of his fellow earthlings lay unconscious in the hull of a heavily modified Clinohumite inter-system cargo ship that was quickly traversing interstellar space on its way back to its home system.

He had hurriedly slipped it on the night a unit of Fleet special duty forces commandeered him and six hundred sixty-one of his fellow earthlings and brought them to the Sthene system[41] inside Realm space.

Now, eleven days later, he still had possession of the jacket and also the Clinohumite issued school notebook he had stowed away in one of its pockets. In fact, he was wearing the jacket as he found a seat in the crowded, but nearly silent, waiting room. He and many of his cowed fellow expatriates had just been firmly escorted by Fleet personnel here to sit and wait in—what was to Teodor—obviously, some kind of government office.

It was in fact, a Realmcustoms center and Teodor and the other earthlings were waiting to be formally processed so that they could begin their new life as visitors to, and later Citizens of, the Realm.

He looked around at the numerous portraits of the beloved Imperial Majesty and mockingly thought to himself, "I can certainly see why the Realm would be enthralled by your beauty. What with your scale clad muzzle, your crocodilian teeth, your shaggy crop of unkempt brownish hair, and your lovely azurite and malachite colored dress complimenting your beady little yellow reptilian eyes. You are certainly a looker!"

Most of the imperial portraits were actually posters extolling the Citizenry to take seriously their many civic duties. Teodor thought that, "Work hard or I'll eat you." might have summed up the whole lot of nonsense rather well.

He slowly unzipped a pocket and retrieved his school notebook. A quick look around assured him that his actions were considered nonthreatening by the soldiers keeping watch over the room. In fact, his personal belongings had already been given a thorough inspection while he was still aboard the Fleet warship, and by now, the contents of his notes were being used to update the understanding the Realm military and security forces had about their pesky little neighbors, the Clinohumites.

He activated the school notebook and began to read over what he had been taught about the non-human races of the Realm. Up to now, all the Realm's Citizens he had seen had been human and he was anxiously hoping to finally see an actual alien.

After endless waiting, he was finally admitted to a dismal

little office and instructed by the room's only occupant to sit down opposite him in a typically uncomfortable chair. For just a moment, Teodor had the dumbest open mouth smile on his face as he looked over at the only non-human 'person' he had ever met in his entire life.

The ettringite remained seated but still managed a smartly executed salute as he gave the Realmgreeting "Our Imperial Majesty!"

Teodor managed to awkwardly give a wrong handed version of the salute as he returned the customary greeting in his own independent way, "*Your* Imperial Majesty!"

The ettringite seemed immune to the affronts to Realm tradition and merely began the official interrogation in his usual manor, "Good day to you. I am Citizen Detlef. Welcome to *The Thenardite Brokered Federation of Planetary Republics and Political Bodies*. Your name, place of birth, and primary occupation, please, visitor?"

"Teodor Korzeniowski. I was born on planet Earth. I am a professional kidnap victim."

"Please, say again, visitor?" the ettringite pleasantly requested with a puzzled look. Teodor was a little surprised at the outcome of *his* first test. These ettringites did not seem to be the human killing monsters that Jutte had told them about. At least this one hadn't yet jumped over the desk and fastened its toothy jaws around his throat. Not that Teodor was complaining, but it did seem he was right about the Clinohumite's ample exaggerations.

Teodor stopped trying to test out his suppositions and explained very truthfully and precisely what had happened to him over the last six or seven months. The ettringite thanked him for the information, and then turning his interface so Teodor could see it, showed him a hundred or so questions and once again made the same simple request, "Your primary occupation is what, Visitor Teodor Korzeniowski?"

So began the longest and most frustrating interview of Teodor's entire life. For hour upon hour, upon hour, Teodor had to, by way of exactly answering totally meaningless questions, try to convince this bureaucratic automaton of just why Teodor Korzeniowski of Utica, New York, United States of America, planet Earth, should be allowed to gain temporary visitor status and be allowed the heady privilege of entering the bureaucratic paradise that was the Realm.

It didn't matter that Teodor had been taken from the Earth to a moon in Clinohumite controlled space by the Realm's enemies. It didn't matter that it had been actual Realm Fleet personnel, acting under the direct orders of their Realm's Imperial Majesty, that had taken him from Breithaupt-Seven and brought him here to the Realm. No, all that mattered to this petty rule-junky was that this human was inside Realm space. That therefore, he obviously must want to stay there and so, again most obviously, he must be required to prove beyond any doubt that he was adequately qualified to gain access to the very place he was now existing in and would like to apply for permission to enter.

Detlef ended his work day at 12:40 hours. Since Teodor had not been able to satisfactorily answer all the questions in the time allotted, he would need to be escorted back to the Fleet controlled area where the earthlings were housed.

"Tomorrow, we will try again, Visitor Teodor Korzeniowski." the pleasant ettringite said encouragingly.

This same procedure was repeated each of the next five days. And each night, Teodor would return to the Fleet holding area, only to find that more of his fellow expatriates had moved on to additional interviews. Some, had even been allowed to go and live in the Realm, apparently at the Imperial Majesty's expense. What was wrong with him?

On his way home on the sixth night after beginning his marathon of unrelenting interviews with his new ettringite best-buddy, Detlef, Teodor was as usual walking between two human Fleet crewpersons. Tonight, they must have begun to feel so sorry for their earthling charge that they violated procedure and stopped at a tavern on their way back to base. After they all enjoyed a little lubrication, they continued on with their walk.

Teodor sarcastically thought to himself, "This was going on far to long. By now I'm getting to know Detlef well enough that *I* should invite *him* out for drinks after work. In a few more days, I could ask him if his sister is currently seeing anyone without sounding too forward."

It really scared him that he even knew Detlef had a sister. Her name was Frauke and she was happily legally mated to a Fleet Second Lieutenant named Ingo. Teodor seemed to remember they had three [children].

"Could it be something from his days on Seven?" he thought. Then he had an idea and so he said out loud in Realmspeak, "That's it!" He had just come to a complete stop and was standing in front of and unconsciously looking up at a poster inviting the Realm's Citizenry to consider service in the Guard as a patriotic and profitable career move. So quite understandably, his two companions thought that Teodor had hit upon the answer to his problems and was seriously considering joining the Realm's security services.

Fleet Crewperson Inerweyde kindly advised, "First things first, Visitor Teodor. They don't let just any Citizen join the Guard. And the operative word here is, *Citizen*."

"Funny, Visitor Teodor, you never struck me as the type that would think of joining the Black Tunics. They're an odd lot, full of 'Death before disloyalty,' 'Unquestioning obedience,' and stuff like that. Not that there is anything wrong with loyalty. I don't mean that!" Fleet Crewperson Cothenghys carefully added, looking around.

"No, I'm not thinking of joining the Guard! I just thought of something that may be holding me back from being allowed to stay as a visitor in the Realm. Maybe someone saw my old Clinohumite instructor flash me this Earth human gesture just as I was going aboard a Fleet transport." Teodor suggested, holding up one thumb. "It's a common gesture on Earth but it does have several meanings. Most commonly it means, 'yes' or 'acceptance.' Less commonly, it can mean, 'you're all right,' or even, 'keep up the good work.' If someone saw the gesture, and if it was then misinterpreted and that misinterpretation was added to my file, then maybe, just maybe, someone thinks I'm actually a clandestine Clinohumite agent."

"You know, Gerben. Our friend here could be right. And supposing he is, considering what a *kripslod* you just made of yourself with all that talk about loyalty and the Guard, I think if any members of the Federal Police meet up with us tonight, we should just light Teodor and be done with it."

"Can we take a vote on that?"

"Sure thing, Teodor, but it will be two to one in any case."

Despite their visit to the tavern earlier, his Fleet escort eventually did manage to get him home safely. Shortly thereafter, he was sound asleep in his Fleet provided bunk.

* * *

The three Guard officers were, once again, carefully reviewing the surveillance records of Visitor Teodor Korzeniowski, Fleet Crewperson Laurens Inerweyde, and Fleet Crewperson Gerben Cothenghys' unofficial visit to a tavern called, *The Engineer's Brace.*

"Guard Captain, we have a certainty level of sixty-nine point four percent."

"All right then. Guard Second Lieutenant Lansol, pass the word to Guard Commander Detlef. Tomorrow, Visitor Teodor Korzeniowski is finished with his first application and can move on to step two."

Chapter Nine
And Then He Met Her!
1756 fTF [2002 CE]

RSDS hub 785/ *Anatase Station*, the Realm

The Realm's government had felt that the kidnapped humans could not be safely repatriated to Earth, and their Realm relations didn't seem to want their impoverished and illiterate kin hanging around their planets, so they were eventually taken to a civilian station orbiting a mainly cerargyrite inhabited planet.

Teodor thought the cerargyrites were somewhat cat-like both physically and in personality. They were inscrutable and aloof. But still, they kept their station impeccably clean and they didn't seem to mind a few hundred Earth-born humans being kept there at the Realm's expense.

Up to this time, he had met a lot of Realm-born humans, a few ettringites, and many cerargyrites, but few, if any, members of the other races of the Galaxy. Then, after a couple of years on station, he finally did get a chance to bump into a member of another race. It was a palagonite and from where he lay on the deck, Teodor thought it looked like a long armed tyrannosaurus wearing a shabby fur coat.

"Sorry to knock you down, Citizen. I didn't see you down there. You should be more careful!" the palagonite said.

"Dumb Ass! Maybe you need glasses, or perhaps an asteroid impact." the human thought. Another species to add to his *list*.

Teodor had always been good at picking up languages and so he was soon better off than his fellow refuges. He could at least leave his room and mingle with the natives. It was on one of those day outings, that he felt a very odd pain growing in his lower back. As the day wore on, the pain grew sharper. He suspected that this could be the result of that fur covered mountain knocking him to the deck just a few days before. He was finding it rather hard to walk.

"Time to take advantage of the Realmcare arraignment — before some do-gooding Citizen decides I need to be put to sleep," he reasoned to himself as he saw more than a few stares from passersby.

The computer at the information kiosk informed him that he could find routine medical assistance customized for his species at a location in block 17659CV-67Z and also kindly provided a map. It was only a five or six minute walk down station so he declined the computer's helpful offer of summoning assistance and decided to walk it unaided. That was a big mistake. By the time he reached the clinic some forty minutes later, he was nearly crawling from the pain.

Even though Teodor was in great pain, he was still able to quickly come to one of his cynical opinions about the place. As he later expressed it, "The clinic was one of those stand in line, cough, move to the next line, veterinary centers so lovingly provided by the resident bureaucratic twits. Medicine administered by Lunch Ladies in a communal cafeteria. Despite being euphemistically referred to as, 'customized for my species,' I appeared to be the only human in the place. The 'Lunch Ladies' seemed to be exclusively cerargyrites, as were their victims. After a few routinely painful and humiliating tests, I was placed in a small examination room and told to wait patiently for my examiner to enter the room. Then, it would undoubtedly proceed to poke, prod, and puncture me into submission."

When the med tech[42] finally entered, Teodor was very much pleasantly surprised. She was obviously overworked, rather pretty, and comfortably human.

She introduced herself as Med Tech Thresher Selverlinck and inquired if he was, "For a certainty: a male human, aged thirty-nine, and born on the planet Earth. Possibly suffering

And Then He Met Her! 61

from a bruised and infected kidney as well as delusional paranoia. Oh, and named Teodor Korzeniowski?" She asked all this without once looking up from his chart.

He replied in the affirmative and searched her hands for any sign of a wedding ring. Forgetting that it was unlikely that a med tech would be wearing one on duty, even if it was a custom practiced by humans in the Realm—which it is not.

"I'm sorry, what was that part about the delusions?" He at last remembered to inquire.

She was very tired and in no mood for [loonies] this late in her shift. "You told the first examiner that you thought the palagonites were trying to have you assassinated." She stated this in the sternest, matronly, no nonsense voice she could muster. All the while she crossed the room and gestured that he recline on the examination table.

The medical diagnostic machine concurred with the first examination, and after checking the instruments, so did Thresher. "Med Tech Thresher Selverlinck has examined the patient and concurs with the findings of medical diagnostic machine, uh ... 76985," she spoke to the room. Then turning her attention to Teodor she asked, "Well, Citizen Teodor Korzeniowski, do you authorize this clinic to undertake treatment for your conditions, and in so doing, to assign liability for costs incurred to the station authorities—in your name?"

"Yes, to treating the kidney—only!" Teodor answered. "About the palagonites, I didn't say they were trying to assassinate me. I said my injury might have been the result of a palagonite *accidentally* knocking me down a few days ago!" Teodor hastily explained. He liked her and was afraid she thought he was a great deal less normal than he was.

"That was careless, Citizen. They are very large. Didn't you see it coming towards you?" scolded Thresher, as she applied treatment devises to his area of discomfort.

"Careless of me! The shaggy behemoth walked right over

me!" She had hit nerve both physically and figuratively and Teodor shouted out his reply.

The room spoke, {"Citizen! Please restrict yourself to civil language. Conversations are monitored in the examination room. Use of additional obscene language could lead to your being instructed to leave these facilities."}

"I didn't use obscene language! I'm from Earth and sometimes the old colloquialisms slip into my conversation." he replied to Thresher in a soft calm voice. She hadn't said anything, but Teodor was very lonely and felt he wanted to, ever so calmly, explain himself to her. "Please, like me!" he thought.

She adjusted the equipment and more or less automatically tried to calm him down by saying in a concerned voice, "It must be very difficult for you, living so far from home." She made more adjustments then asked, "Was it a male or a female who knocked you down?"

"I'm sorry, while I was laying down there, I failed to take inventory." He tried a little humor and a friendly smile.

She liked the smile and was beginning to like the man, but thought it wasn't yet time to respond favorably to his humor. "I didn't ask if you gave it a physical. Can't you tell them apart just at a glance?" Now, a little more painful adjusting of the equipment and a long time reading the instruments. "Was it about two and a half times your height? Or less?"

"Less. About three meters or so. Maybe five hundred kilograms." Teodor answered.

She removed some of the devices. Then stepped back with a happy look and said "Well, that makes it a male, unless it was still a little girl. The adult females are much larger. Four meters or better and at least twice a male's weight. My old professor at university explained it's from all the extra plumbing they have to carry, being egg layers and that. Your kidney is all fixed up. I'll let you rest a bit. When I return, I'll remove the rest of the equipment and you can be on your way, Citizen." She turned to go.

"They lay eggs? I didn't know that. I wonder what else I don't know about sex in the Realm." He tried to be coy, but came across desperate.

She tried to keep things on a professional medical level and so she replied, "Palagonites lay eggs and produce milk for their hatchlings. Well, I guess that would make them prototheriums. Halotrichites are reptiles—eggs but no milk. Ettringites and cerargyrites are placental mammals like us. Those are the only member species that I've ever worked with."

Teodor was hoping she wouldn't have to leave, so he asked what she knew about thenardites.

"We never studied them in school. Really no point, there are only a handful left in the continuüm and I read once that they never need medical assistance. A very strange creature by all accounts. We did have one stop by and give a guest lecture in one of my history classes. It was retired Guard Admiral Wilymia Alphrontex. He's one of the only ones you see around the Realm anymore. You know it's funny, but I can't even remember if the Guard admiral was introduced as he or she. I think they may all be *it*."

He tried again with a joke and a smile, "Hard to get little thenardites if they're all *it*. I think you would occasionally need a *he* and a *she*."

"There are no little ones, just the retired Guard admiral and one or two others. It's sad to think they're just dying out as a species."

It took a few more minutes, but in the end, Thresher agreed to go out to dinner with Teodor. At least nature was still taking its course among humans.

Teodor Korzeniowski was at last, a very happy man.

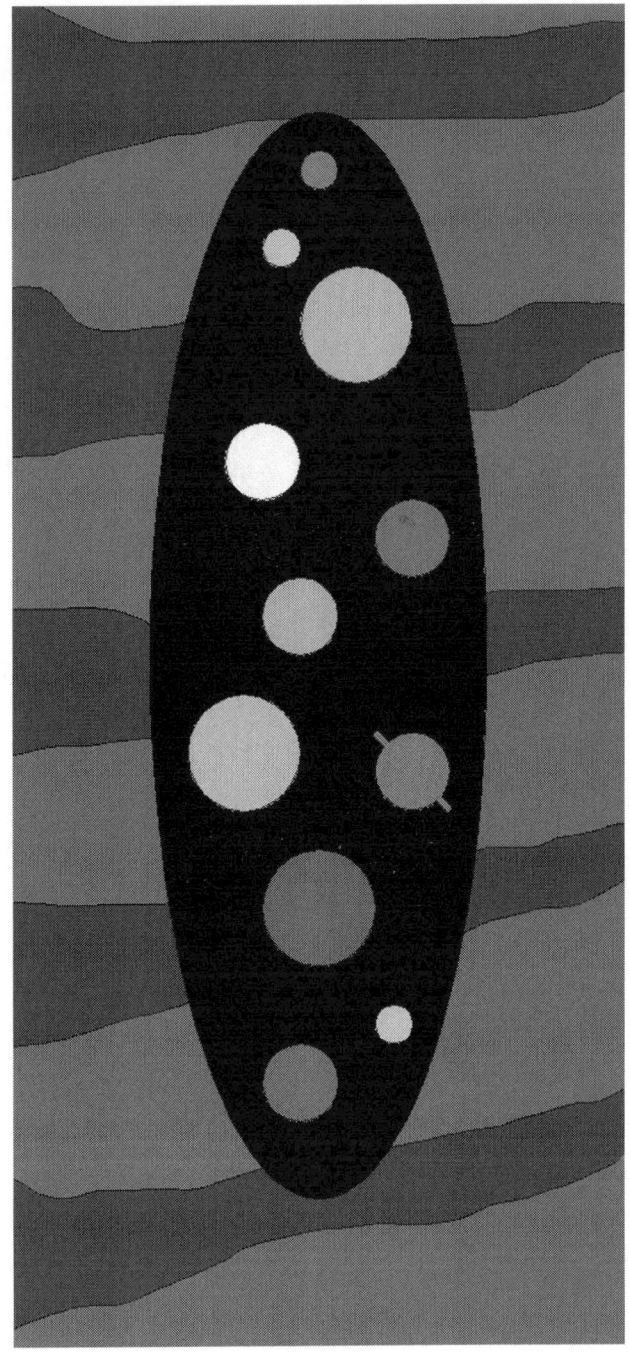

Fig.2. Black and white copy of the Realm's official emblem.

Chapter Ten
Above the Waters of Palagon

Palagon Station, Proculus System, the Realm
1758 fTF

"*Palagon Station* was one of the busiest places one could find anywhere in the Realm. Citizens from the various member planets, visitors from the far reaches of the Galaxy, permanent residents and transients, all packed together high above the blue seas and brown green continents of planet Palagon. Each one had a story, and when their stories intertwined in less than peaceful ways, that's when I get involved. Name's Stanislav Endicott. I'm a security agent, says so on my identity card—"

"Teodor, what are you doing?"
"Sorry, Thresher, just working out a story in my head. You were saying?"
"I was saying, this is Cerdic-Chaidam Academy. Why don't you wait here while I go in for my interview?"
"That's fine. It looks like a good place to sit over there. ... We both know you'll get the job this time. I love you and I'll see you soon, *Liebchen*.[43] I'll wait right over there."

Teodor and Thresher had been legally mated for just over two years. They were still very much in love, but times were tough and you can't eat love. You still need to work to pay the bills, even in the Realm. The problem for them was Teodor, or more to the point, the fact that Teodor was from Earth. Being a refugee he did get a little financial help from the government, but that wouldn't have supported him if he lived alone in an old shipping container.[44] He was far from lazy, but with no practical skills no one would hire him. In a world filled with robots and automation there was little use for living, sentient, deck cleaners. He tried his hand at writing, but here, his speculative fiction stories were just silly. His [romances][45] and adventure stories were out of touch with currant fashions, and who would read travel guides about a planet no one was allowed to visit. A lot of his fellow refugees acquired positions lecturing at universities about their experiences on Earth and with the Clinohumites, but unfortunately for Teodor, there were only so many universities in the Realm. For the first time in his life Teodor wished he could be back working in his old cubical. Anything to have a way to help support Thresher.

It wasn't that much easier for her. Thresher was a daughter [of Fleet veterans] and as such had received her education at reduced expense. But grateful as the Realm might be for her parents' past sacrifices, they weren't going to help her get into any but the lowest cost schools. So, after graduation, she found herself working as a med tech on transfer [shipping] stations, agri plants, and mining sites. You don't support two adult humans with the pay you get patching up miners and farmers under Realmcare.

There was one additional problem that our young couple were only vaguely concerned about—that was Teodor's big mouth. You would think that someone as concerned of what he saw as the totalitarian underpinnings of the Realm would keep quietly in the background. Not Teodor Korzeniowski. No, he would open his mouth and say the stupidest things in front of all the wrong people. Political officers, security agents, and surveillance computers, they had all been privileged to be witness to Teodor's [soap box dissertations.] [46] His mate patently put up with his 'insightful' views about all things Realm. She had even lovingly tried to convince him of what she thought to be the careful view of the society around them. It never worked. It's hard to convince someone that your government isn't oppressive, when you have to whisper. So he kept on [spouting,][47] and she kept on looking for a job.

Up to this time, the truly grandest of all his badly timed outpourings and the stupidest of all his stupid comments, he had saved for the worst of the worst times he could ever have found to open his big mouth. Then, it almost cost his mate a good deal more than the security clearance she needed to land a good job.

Walpurg Station, Ulexite System, the Realm 1757 fTF

It was about eight months[48] before he stood beside a pedestrian way on *Palagon Station,* thinking up the opening lines of that detective story he always meant to write. As usual, Teodor and Thresher were on a station. And as usual she was looking for a job and he was feeling that he had let her down. What was different, this time, was that this was not a civilian station out in the [backwaters.] No, this was a military station orbiting a populous member planet. This was Federal Territory. The home location for the High Court of the Judiciary. How Teodor and Thresher managed to be on this station, at this inopportune time, is one of those unforeseen occurrences that haunt the dreams of dutiful secret police personnel the continuüm over. For this was the day the Imperial Majesty [Empress Caesellia], Chief Executive of *The Thenardite Brokered Federation of Planetary Republics and Political Bodies,* was to receive the graduating class of the Guard Officers Training School.

Thresher came out of the building and met her husband waiting in the [mall].[49]

"How'd it go, *Liebchen?*" he asked her, trying to sound encouraging.

"I didn't get the job. I just wasn't qualified." she answered with a strangely happy tone to her voice.

"They were that blunt? Poor, dear one. You never get a break. I wish I could tell them—"

"Oh, no, he was very kind," she interrupted. "Let's talk and walk. I'm too exited to stand around."

"That's fine with me. Now, tell me the good news."

"The man who interviewed me was an old friend of Dad's. They served together on the *Skyfish*. He said he thought he recognized the name and so, since I was already on station, he would let me interview. No chance though. Assistant med tech at an agri complex. Exclusively halotrichites. No job for a human!"

"Halotrichites don't like humans? Or do they like humans too much? Maybe, on toasted bread with a dipping sauce on the side." he asked.

"Teodor! That's not funny! They're not like that. Halotrichites are nice. I told you about Gree.[50] She was great to be around. ... Let's stop here for something?" Thresher had found a vendor with her favorite quick-to-get food.

Teodor didn't remember Gree, but then again Thresher was always telling him about this or that school friend. He seemed to remember Frida was the one who knocked a professor's lunch into his lap in the cafeteria. Or was that Halla? No, Halla was the one that blacked out a whole dorm trying to re-wire the door sensor so they could sneak out after curfew. He took a guess, "Was Gree the one who burned a hole in the floor?"

"No! That was Fuzzi Eck'crawd. I don't think Gree ever did anything wrong. She was just the type everyone liked. Happy—always dancing around. I think she married an artist and lives on Hauyn Primary now. I hope she's still happy. ... Happy, like I am with you." she thoughtfully added.

"Ah ha. All right then, what's wrong with halotrichites?" he asked as he hopped up onto a bench made for palagonites and pulled her up next to him.

"Do you remember that Citizen you saw when we were dating? The one that was running with his head down low, his tail straight out, and his hands held close in—like this? We were still living on that RSDS[51] Hub. Remember? You couldn't stop staring at it. You said it reminded you of something that used to live back on Earth."

"The dinosaur? Yes, I remember. That was a halotrichite? [Man!] could that thing move. And, Grandmother, what very big claws you have."

"That's the problem with with human med techs treating halotrichites. Even when they remember to keep their nails capped—and I never knew one that did—they can still send you flying if you sneak up on them. They don't mean it of course, just jumpy. Apologies don't mean much when, ... Well, think about what you could do to me if I surprised you when you were in bed sleeping?"

Teodor started to answer her with a dirty little grin.

"Stow your gear! That's not what I'm talking about. You might instinctively lash out and give me a split lip or a black eye. Surprise a halotrichite and you could get torn wide open. No thanks! I don't have the training to work on halotrichites. I'll stick to safer patients and to safer environments. Halotrichites also like to keep the heat up quite a bit. Not so bad on stations, that's pretty steady, but planetside—wow! I remember the time we all went off station—it was to a little moon that the parents of one of the girls had a vacation place on. You should have seen Gree! Bundled up in about six layers. She looked like one of those characters in the old water rescue videos. No, we'll do all right. We aren't that bad off yet."

Teodor was relieved to see his wife so happy. Things hadn't been going that well lately. "But damn it, she's right! We're not that bad off." he thought, reasoning with himself. "I still get my allowance from Momma Government and Thresher did manage to find work—eventually. Not the best work , but not risking disembowelment either."

They hopped off the bench and continued up station. Thresher seamed to know the way, and, when she headed back to their rented room to tidy herself up, he knew she had plans.

"So, you still haven't told me why you're in such a good mood. I hear the Imperial Majesty is in town. Invited over for wine and cheese are we? I'll probably be the only male there not wearing a tail." Teodor always laced his speech with [earthisms] when he got silly, and seeing his wife so happy was making him very silly indeed.

"You're close. Look at these!" she excitedly giggled, as she handed him some [tickets.] "Two free passes into the Guard graduation tonight!" Dad's old Fleet buddy had them for important clients, but he didn't end up using them all, so he gave these to us! Imagine that, Teodor! We're going to see our Imperial Majesty. I mean, really see her! Not just on the screens, but in person!"

Teodor wished now that he had taken drama in school. He wanted so much to show his mate that he was as exited as she was—but he wasn't. He despised the Imperial Majesty and every repressive principle she stood for. Nobody elected her—she ruled by right of birth. She had the Guard, her own private little army, wrapped tightly around her to protect herself from any draft of public dissatisfaction. She was a tyrant, a bully, an *élitist*, and she probably kicked [blind puppies.] Blazes! She probably ate them! All he could say was, "Isn't that great, *Liebchen*! Where is the graduation being held?"

* * *

Three hours later, they entered the stadium. Seating one hundred ninety-seven thousand, the athletic stadium the Guard used for its ceremonies was one of the largest in the Realm. Teodor had never been comfortable in crowds and this was almost overwhelming for him. The sight of so many Guard personnel (which he always equated with the Earth's more notorious secrete police) didn't help.

Thresher seemed to, as she did most things, take it in stride. After they passed though the security scanners and entered the seating area, Teodor jokingly asked her if she knew how many of her old school chums were at this moment in the stadium. Thresher replied, that if the lights stayed on, she knew of at least one that wasn't here. With his wife by his side, Teodor felt that even this night would be tolerable.

One advantage of living in a galactic society governed, for the most part, by creatures ten times your body mass, is that, as humans, you find the theater seats quite roomy. Because the tickets they possessed were originally purchased for important clients of any species they had been by necessity reserved in the palagonite-sized seating area. This gave Teodor the idea of stretching out across his seat and napping through the political speeches. He promised Thresher he would wake in time for the book burning. She briefly thought of the advise her friends had given her against having anything to do with him.

Teodor Korzeniowski did not actually carry out his threat of reclining across his seat. For all his faults, Teodor was not stupid. Even in his most rebellious mood, the sight of so many palagonites sitting around him would have set him on his best behavior. Not that even his best behavior would have satisfied his neighbors if they had any concept of what half of the words slipping carelessly from his lips really meant. If they thought about the two humans sitting in their midst at all, it was just puzzled amusement that The One would have ever creäted sentient creatures so small and so delicate. It was *truly* an amazing continuüm.

The lighting arrays built into the stadium began their slow dimming to night mode—a replication of twilight on

Palagon. Now, Teodor understood why Thresher had insisted on their both bringing jackets. The thermostats seamed to be linked with the artificial nightfall and it was getting decidedly chilly. A quick look out of the corners of his eyes showed him that his palagonite neighbors found the conditions very soothing.

All was quiet now, and all eyes were on the great empty field in the center of the vast amphitheater. All eyes that is, with the exception of those belonging to a hatchling sitting with a large female in the row behind him. The little one was staring at Teodor very intently. Its open mouth revealing a row of shiny brand new teeth freshly broken out from the gums.

Teodor whispered to his wife, "Thresher? With palagonites, which comes first, a switch over to solid food or the knowledge that society frowns on you eating your fellow Citizens no matter how tasty they look? ... Never mind, problem solved." The hatchling was obviously with its mother. It had snuggled into her fur and was intently licking the milk from her mammary glands. "Would make a nice picture for a [Mother's Day][52] [card.]" Teodor said out loud, but Thresher didn't respond, she was entranced by the spectacle unfolding on the field below.

The music had started and an assortment of Guard personnel had solemnly entered the field from multiple openings scattered under the seating area. They carried torches, and they illuminated the area, as they took their positions facing inward while encircling the field.

Now, onto the field marched group after group of Guard and Fleet personnel. They marched in a strange pattern. When Teodor asked Thresher about this peculiar style of formation, the palagonite in the seat adjoining hers informed him it was called a 'Crystal Formation' and that like a zinc oxide crystal its pattern was necessitated by the great variety in the physical sizes of the participants. Teodor thanked him and made a mental note to keep his voice down.

The field below him was now filled with alternating polygons of light gray clad Fleet and sable clad Guard. In the walkways between the groups there were more torch bearers.

In front of all the troops, and just in front of the stairs leading up to the Imperial box, was a empty platform with more stairs leading from it down onto the field. From an area under the stands, on the side opposite the Imperial Majesty' box, came a very strange creature. It looked basically human or ettringite in shape, but it had a striped lower back and rather halotrichite like tail and hands. It walked down the central path and up one human sized set of stairs onto the platform. Two others—a palagonite female and an ettringite with cropped ears—both dressed as members of the Guard, followed some distance behind it and joined it on the platform. Now, a series of large video screens placed above the seating areas powered up and began presenting a close-up picture of what was occurring on the platform.

Enlarged so that he could see it better, Teodor felt that the creature with the stripes was possibly the scariest looking thing he had ever seen outside of a movie theater. Like most of the other Citizens now joining it on the platform the strange creature was in a version of a Guard uniform.[53]

An [orchestral fanfare] sounded as the Imperial Majesty entered through a door at the back of her box.

All present rose as one and from nearly every mouth in the stadium rang out the Realmgreeting, "Our Imperial Majesty!"

She stood looking down towards her loyal Citizenry for just a moment, returned their salutes, and then descended the stairs to the platform on the field below.

Now the stadium was absolutely silent. You could almost hear, 'the platters in Teodor's brain spin wildly as he overclocked his processors,' or at least that's what he imagined it must have sounded like to Thresher and the others seated around him. Suddenly, he realized that he was standing. He didn't remember doing it. He must have instinctively risen when his wife did. Just then, the little children of several species came skipping up the walkways with flowers for their beloved Imperial Majesty.

"Black uniforms, torches, and flower bearers? Who wrote this crap?" he said out loud as he sat down and started thinking.

The mother palagonite leaned over and asked in a very concerned voice if he was all right.

"Yes. Thank you. Just a little overwhelmed."

"Well, the introductions are over—things will quiet down a bit. Now the graduates will be receiving their daggers." she reassured him as she disentangled her sleeping hatchling from her fur. "Maybe, my mate should get you some cold water. Julius, could you be a dear and fetch these Citizens something cold to drink?"

"No really, thank you very much, but we're fine. Really, we're fine. Aren't you, Thresher?"

Thresher finally realized that she and her mate—mostly her mate—were the local center of attention. "Teodor, nothings wrong is it?" Then, to the concerned palagonites, "Thank you so much! You are very kind, Citizens, but my mate—well, this is just his first time at so solemn an event. He'll be fine. I'll keep an eye on him. Thank you! And thank, *you*, also!" Turning back to Teodor, she whispered, "See! I told you they were gentle beings. Keep this in mind the next time you think they just want to put us out on hunting reserves, or any of that other crap you always worry about. I'm sorry, Teodor. I'm just not used to standing out at public events. Will–You–Please, just sit there quietly."

For the next hour or so, the newly commissioned Guard officers filed out before their Imperial Majesty and the other dignitaries. One by one they saluted the Imperial Majesty and then stood in front of the ettringite officer (with the cropped ears) who had come to the platform just behind that strange looking creature with the stripes.

Teodor overheard some of his neighbors chatting, "This year they swear the Guard oath and receive their dagger from Guard Senior Admiral Sir Maike. My mate's brother's son received his last year, from High Admiral Karen itself. We were all so proud of him. I can still hear his vigorous, manly voice, "I will obey the [Constitution] and the Protocols. I will loyally serve and protect our Imperial Majesty and the institutions and Citizens of *The Thenardite Brokered Federation of Planetary Republics and Political Bodies*, until my duty is fulfilled or my life is ended!" Do you have anyone graduating? Your daughter next year. Oh, it will be so exciting. You get to sit right down in front—almost on the field!"

An adult halotrichite with several young surrounding it was quietly escorted onto the platform. They were supplied with a bench and sat, over on the side, out of the way of the ceremony. The screen panned over and focused in on the Imperial Majesty and the creature with the stripes standing next to her. They both turned and acknowledged the halotrichite family with a bow of their heads.

Teodor stretched over and whispered to Thresher, "Who is that officer next to the Imperial Majesty? I've never seen anything like it."

"It's a thenardite. Probably, Guard Admiral Wilymia Alphrontex, but I can't be sure. I've never seen a rank insignia like that."[54] she whispered back.

"No wonder they're dying out. Who would want to mate with that!" This he said in a whisper that fortunately his wife could not hear. To himself he thought, "And it looks nothing like the pictures dear old Schoonemacker showed us back on Seven."

The last of the graduates returned to the field in front of the platform and now the thenardite gave them a [pep talk.] At least that is what it looked like from where the two humans were sitting. Teodor thought that the ceremony must be winding down. He was running though his mind all the things he would need to say to Thresher—to apologize for the way he acted and the incident he caused. But hold it! There seemed to be something else happening. The Imperial Majesty had walked back to the halotrichite family and taking the adult's hand, had escorted them to the front of the platform. She was now bending very low and hugging and nuzzling each of the five halotrichite children. The thenardite walked over and presented a box to the Imperial Majesty, who in turn, reached into the box and retrieving a medal, placed it around the neck of the adult halotrichite. The screens zoomed in on the medal and Teodor turned to Thresher. He was going to say that it looked just like the one she kept in her jewelry box, but then he stopped. Thresher had her face in her hands and was crying.

The palagonite mother reached over and petted her. "Someone close?" the palagonite asked Teodor.

"I'm not certain, but I think her father received a medal like that after her mother died." he replied. That's really all he knew. Thresher had always changed the subject when he asked her about it.

"Dear one, you're not alone. We're all family." the palagonite mother assured her.

Thresher was regaining her composure. She stood up and kissed her comforter on the nose. When she did, the hatchling reached over and started playing with her hair.

* * *

Thresher was herself again and even laughing a little, as she and Teodor left the stadium about an hour later.

Chapter Eleven
Guard Admiral Reinier

Aegerite Station, Proculus System, the Realm

Guard Admiral Reinier was the commanding officer of the Political Police and he loved order. A story often told by his subordinates was that he was incapable of walking through the officer's mess without stopping to arrange all the condiments on every table to exact symmetry. That the story was never repeated to his face probably means it was greatly exaggerated. Nonetheless, pity the poor investigating agent that turned in a report that was less than perfect.

Guard Captain Evert always felt his reports were thorough and professional. And, although he had recently become aware of a growing disillusion with his department's responsibilities and nearly with the Guard's duties in general, he still felt no reason to doubt his performance on this occasion.

Evert had been waiting with increasing impatience outside Guard Admiral Reinier's office for well over three hours before finally being allowed in.

After exchanging the Realmgreeting and, in addition, the ettringite specific greeting, the Guard admiral returned to his seat and gestured for Evert to take a seat himself.

"How did things go at the graduation, Guard Captain?"

"Guard Admiral, I am pleased to inform you that there were no incidents worth reporting."

"And incidents not worth reporting?" The Guard admiral asked with a smile.[55] He knew he had a reputation of being rather harsh with his junior officers and had 'modified his course' in an attempt to change his image. He led a spotless life, but it did no one in power any good to have your underlings endlessly searching for information that could bring about your ruïnation.

"Very little, Guard Admiral. A human on the watch list managed to gain access to the proceedings. He was closely monitored and there were no difficulties." Guard Captain Evert said and then thinking it would be unwise to appear to be hiding anything quickly continued, "The matter has been investigated. A local agri supplier by the name of Coorenwinder Passchyer was interviewing a transient med tech for a job. Citizen Passchyer found out that this med tech, a human female named Thresher Korzeniowski,[56] was the daughter of retired Fleet Chief Crewperson Carsteloot Selverlinck. Citizen Passchyer and the senior Selverlinck served in the Fleet together for eighteen years. He gave her two of ten tickets to the graduation that he had purchased originally to encourage goodwill with some of his customers." He looked down again at his report to give the Guard admiral time to let the trivialness of the incident seep in. "The med tech, Thresher Korzeniowski, has no record of suspect activities, but for the last two years has been the legal mate of an Earth-born human male, Teodor Korzeniowski. He was one of the Earth-born humans taken captive by the Clinohumites approximately five years ago. That past association with the Clinohumites and a propensity to vocally find fault with Realm customs and authorities, has placed him on the watch list. The two humans sat together throughout the ceremony. They were closely monitored. There were no incidents. Both are still on *Walpurg Station*. She has gone on several additional job interviews in the last thirty-six hours, but has yet to find employment."

"May I see the report, Guard Captain." It was not a question. The Guard admiral reached out and took the report tablet from the Guard captain's hand. Guard Admiral Reinier put the repositioning of his image on hold indefinitely.

Guard Admiral Reinier quickly skimmed over the text, then, with growing disbelief at his junior's sudden incompetence, he asked, "They discussed turning off the lights in the stadium? You don't find that worth reporting, Guard Captain?"

"Guard Admiral, you will *please* note the context. The female human was replying to what the surveillance system interpreted as a mildly sarcastic question asked her by her mate. We investigated her background and see this as a reference to an incident that occurred during her training to be a med tech some fifteen years ago.[57] One of her fellow dorm residents had a casual mate off-campus and in an attempt to enable her to circumvent curfew, an ettringite named Frida—also a resident of the dorm—inadvertently disabled the lighting system in the dorm building. The university authorities investigated the matter and those involved with the situation were reprimanded. We concluded that the reference to this event in her life was intended to be humorous."

"Humorous? This ettringite female ... Frida. Has she been investigated, Guard Captain?"

"Yes, sir."

"And what were the findings, Guard Captain?"

"She graduated from university with an advanced medical qualification. She was excepted to the Guard Offers Training School and graduated with honors five years ago. Medical Officer Guard First Lieutenant Frida is currently serving aboard the IGSS *Eviscerator*. We checked with both the ship's commanding officer and with the political officer. Both report her to be a fine young officer with no questionable contacts or activities. Also, Guard Admiral ... Medical Officer Guard First Lieutenant Frida[58] ... is my daughter. You will find in my report a request that I be transferred off this investigation. I believe that is standard procedure under the circumstances, sir?"

"It is. Thank you, Guard Captain Evert, I will read your report, thoroughly, and then I will get back to you."

"Guard Admiral?"

"A question, Guard Captain?"

"A request, sir. The records indicate that the human Teodor Korzeniowski often criticizes the security services of the Realm for what he sees as overly harsh and oppressive tactics. Please, don't let him be proved right in his own case."

"Guard Captain Evert, you may return to your duty station. Our Imperial Majesty!"

Guard Captain Evert hastily rose, saluted and returned the Realmgreeting, "Our Imperial Majesty!"

The Guard admiral looked down at the report and began reading, then growled out an order to the exiting Guard captain, "Send Guard Commander Sascha up to see me — right away."

Guard Captain Evert left the Guard admiral's office without speaking another word. There was no longer any need to. He had tried to help his daughter's school friend and her *kripslod* of a mate. Now, he would gather-up the consequences.

He stopped in the Guard admiral's outer office just long enough to trade [halfhearted] pleasantries with Guard First Lieutenant Felix. The palagonite reminded him of one of the junior partners at that firm he apprenticed at during his [senior year] in law school. He had been so happy working there until a position in the Guard had tempted him away.

Now, Evert thought about his [turbulent] relationships with Guard Admiral Rainier and before that with his highly esteemed predecessor Guard Admiral Wilymia Alphrontex. Connecting the two thoughts in his mind he questioned, "I wonder if I did the right thing back then? Klara might have been happier if I was practicing law on some nice quiet station out on the frontier. I know I would!"

Chapter Twelve
A Visit from Parent

Guard Operations Center-Palagon
Planet Palagon, Proculus System, the Realm

Guard First Ensign Sonja came back from showing her superior's visitor where to wait and returned to her desk outside in the corridor. When she had joined the Guard she had never dreamed that one day she would be an aide to the highest officer in the Realm. It was a great honor for one just out of Guard Officer Training School, but it was still quite embarrassing to have to sit behind a little desk out in the main corridor on the [first floor] of the massive planetside edifice that was Guard Operations Center-Palagon. One of High Admiral Karen's long-term aides had explained the reasons for this conspicuous perch, but Sonja still didn't fully understand. To her it was humiliating, and more than a little unnerving, to have hundreds of Fleet and Guard officers, and governmental ministers walking past her everyday.

She couldn't fault the view though. Just four meters past her desk was the transparent barrier that protected pedestrian traffic from the long and wide opening to the [ground level,] the [arcades], and still further down to the transport station in the buildings lowest public level. Above the level she was on and up through the protected shaft were the views of the twenty-nine additional levels of the building. At the very top, and just discernible from where Sonja sat, was the great transparent roof that let natural light, but not the planet's weather, fall deep down inside the structure. Today, a thunderstorm raged outside, but the young female ettringite could sit warm and dry, with her departmentally approved cup of *fortesgrr*[59] close at hand, awaiting the arrival of her thenardite superior.

She didn't have to wait long. It was still quite early and so the corridor was nearly deserted. That gave Sonja a uninterrupted view down to the lifts, and after just sitting down and beginning to enjoy her beverage, she noticed the [caramel] furred, black nosed muzzle, and white trimmed rounded ears of her quadrupedal boss. If there was any doubt as to the species of creature that was coming towards her down the corridor, it was eliminated by the sight of the thenardite's seventeen brown dorsal stripes and stiff tail.

High Admiral Karen must have picked up the odor of its early visitor, for just as it reached a respectable and shoutless distance from its aide, it stopped and, raising its left manus, greeted the now standing ettringite with, "Our Imperial Majesty. Good morning, Guard First Ensign Sonja. You are in good health and [spirits,] I trust?"

"Our Imperial Majesty! Thank you, High Admiral, I am. And good morning to you."

"Have you shown my parent, retired Guard Admiral Wilymia Alphrontex, into my office and provided it with refreshments?"

"I showed the retired Guard admiral to a seat in your outer office, sir. ... I'm afraid I neglected to arrange for any refreshments. ... I only just got my *fortesgrr* a few moments ago. ... I'm very sorry, High Admiral."

"You're forgiven, Guard First Ensign. It's early in the day. But let's rectify that omission expediently, shall we?"

"Immediately, High Admiral!"

"Send down to catering and have them send up an ample selection of raw organ meats and some *sorenton* tea. Is my parent in a bipedal or a quadrupedal configuration?"

"Ah, ... bipedal, High Admiral."

"Then have the tea served in a cup with warmed *drocalli* milk on the side. Thank you, Sonja. Bring it in as soon as it arrives."

Sonja opened her superior's door and then, after closing it

behind the High Admiral, felt she could breathe again. "Forgetting to provide the Protector of the Realm's visitors with refreshments. Worse, its own parent. That's a mistake I'll never make again!" Sonja thought to herself as she communicated through to catering.

Once inside its office, the High Admiral exchanged the Realmgreeting with its parent and then, after engaging in a few niceties of social convention, invited the retired Guard admiral to join it in its private office.

"I'm very sorry, Parent. Guard First Ensign Sonja is new here and still rather inexperienced."

"I would think that any Citizen of our Realm, young or old, would understand common courtesy and not have to have each and every one of its duties detailed. Disgraceful. What kind of hatchlings are being raised in our society—It boggles the mind to contemplate. She didn't forget her own precious *fortesgrr*. I can smell it from here."

"Again, I'm sorry, Parent."

"Tymorann told me that you were just the same back when you were a child. You must remember, Karen, that they are your servants, not your friends. I suppose, you will have a gentle talk with the young ettringite. All is forgiven with good spleened, *Tante* Karen.[60] Personally, I'd bust her down to Guard crewperson and maybe then she'd learn a little lesson about taking her job seriously. It is a *privilege* to serve the Protector of the Realm, not a *given* from The One."

About this time Sonja entered with the refreshments, "Excuse me, Excellencies. Should I put this over on your desk or on the table?"

"Here on the table. Thank you, Sonja. As you have undoubtedly overheard my parent's chastisement, I feel I can add nothing further—except, that you must pay closer attention to your duties and be glad you still have them. That is all, Guard First Ensign. Our Imperial Majesty."

"Our Imperial Majesty!" returned the ettringite. Then she

left and closed both the inner and outer doors behind her.

"Parent, I appreciate your desire to improve my staff and to help me fulfill my obligations to our Realm, but please understand my position. I am the first Protector of the Realm in over six hundred years. I'm certain that more than half the Realm's Citizens think that I could have them executed for just looking at me without a sufficiently warm smile. And they're right, I could. I have the power of life and death over every Citizen of our Realm — of course with the exception of our Imperial Majesty — "

"Including our Imperial Majesty." Wilymia corrected.

"Including our Imperial Majesty, Parent. But I have never enjoyed that kind of power. I do enjoy fulfilling my duties and my obligations as The One gives me strength. I will weed out corruption and treason without fear or dishonesty. But! I will not terrorize the free-born Citizen's of *The Thenardite Brokered Federation of Planetary Republics and Political Bodies*, a government that you and Uncle Tymorann were instrumental in bringing into existence."

"Then perhaps we should get down to business, Karen. And then I can get back to Anker and this year's meadowball season." retired Guard Admiral Alphrontex said as it walked over and secured the doors. It then turned its attention to the building's security system, "Computer, identify me."

{"You are a thenardite. A more detailed identification is not possible, or required at this time."}

"Computer, as regards this room only and without your indicating it elsewhere, or remembering it later — I, by the right of my race, invoke the Eighth Protocol. Deäctivate all monitoring of this room and secure it from all intrusion until a thenardite commands you to do otherwise. Is that understood, Computer?"

{"It is understood, Lord!"}

"Parent, was that necessary?"

"Let's hope not, Offspring. ... Karen, do you know what

religious beliefs your ineffective young Guard first ensign subscribes to?"

"I have never concerned myself with the religion or the race of my subordinates, but I'm ready and willing to be educated as to why I should."

"The *Cult of Adalheidis* has returned and King Leudoberct [of Ettring] intends to use it for his own nationalistic objectives. From this moment on you must begin to thoroughly purge the Guard of any and all Citizen's that place their allegiance to religion, or to race, above their allegiance to the Realm. Specifically, I'm referring to our ettringite Citizens, but additional investigations will reveal what they reveal."

"Do you have any suspicions, Parent?"

"Guard Admiral Reinier has five ettringite members of his headquarters staff at the Department of the Political Police. Three, he has *personally* appointed to their current assignments. Of those, Guard Commander Sascha and Guard Second Lieutenant Hrolf are traitors working directly for the *Cult of Adalheidis*.

"Twenty-five days ago, Reinier took exception to the comments of another ettringite on his staff—one Guard Captain Evert. Reinier had him reassigned as the political officer at a RealmRock mine in the Wolnyn System.

"Two points are of interest in this matter—two seemingly contradictory points. First, the mine site will soon be in possession of several mining charges of a type that the *Cult of Adalheidis* plan to use in an assassination attempt on our Imperial Majesty. Second, Guard Captain Evert is reported to be of a secular frame of mind. His father, Poldi, was an ardent [evangelist] for the *Way of The One*. He was also a close friend of your Uncle Tymorann. ... So, is Evert working for the Realm, or is he working for the *Cult of Adalheidis*? You must find that out, Karen."

"And what about Guard Admiral Reinier?"

"His mother is a significant contributor to the *Cult of Adalheidis* and is reported to be an ardent anti-human. One can not choose one's family, so we should not necessarily hold that against the Guard admiral. Still, we must thoroughly investigate Reinier. And if he is a supporter of the *Cult of Adalheidis* ... then he will need to disappear. It is the only way to deal with traitors so highly placed."

"If he is indeed a traitor, Parent."

"He's meeting with you tomorrow, isn't he?"

"Yes. He has concerns about an Earth-born human that showed up at the Guard graduation last month."

"How very convenient. I wonder what Sibling Tymorann would make of that chance occurrence?"

"How is Uncle?"

"As religious as always. It disapproves of my continuing to meddle about in politics. It strongly feels that this constitutes disloyalty to The One and the Divine State with which it believes The One will soon grace all creätion. Your Uncle escapes reality into religious daydreams far too readily. Recently, I had hoped it would contact a few of its friends in the Clinohumite Republic and help get that nation's leaders to join us at the negotiating table."

"Uncle was unwilling?"

"As the earthling's say, 'Like pulling teeth!' getting it to use its contacts to get anything worthwhile done."

"Perhaps now that its old friend, Dame Odelie Hutenburch, has been elected President of the Supreme—"

"Perhaps, but I wouldn't expect it, Karen. One other matter of utmost importance. Be *very* careful how you deal with Fleet Admiral Sigsteinn. He's dirty, but just how dirty remains to be seen. For now, leave him to me. If we spook him he's likely to make a grand exit and perhaps take a lot of innocent Citizens with him. I'll keep you posted on my investigations and preparations."

"Very good, Parent."

Chapter Thirteen
Gin and Tonic

Guard Operations Center-Palagon
Planet Palagon, Proculus System, the Realm

The music coming from the inner-office finally stopped at length, indicating that that the High Admiral could once again be safely disturbed. The aide got up from her desk and walked through the outer office and past the ever more restlessly waiting Guard admiral. She gently opened the Protector of the Realm's door, and putting her head in she suggested, "Excellency? Just a reminder, Guard Admiral Reinier is still waiting to see you. May I show him in now?" This was a very old-fashioned way of performing her duty, but when dealing with the High Admiral, old fashioned ways are usually the best ways.

The Protector of the Realm gave its consent and the aide informed the Guard admiral that the High Admiral would see him now.

Guard Admiral Reinier took just the shortest moment to collect himself and then entered the office. It was the first time he had ever visited the High Admiral's office and, had he let himself, he could almost have stared in amazement. Even on a planet this room was an anachronism. Polished wood floors, wood wainscoting, plaster walls hung with paintings, and to top it all off what looked to be a plastered ceiling. Around the edges of the room were pieces of furniture that appeared to be made out of wood. On the furniture was arranged haphazardly (and therefore to Reinier quite upsetting) an eclectic selection of small decorative items and several strange mechanical devices. In the center of the room was a large wooden desk littered with printed documents. Behind the desk on an un-padded wooden chair sat the Protector of the Realm itself.

The Guard admiral fervently saluted, "Our Imperial Majesty!"

The High Admiral returned the salute. "Our Imperial Majesty. Good day, Guard Admiral Reinier, how may I be of service?" It asked in a cheerful and quiet voice.

"High Admiral, this will only take a little of your time."

The Protector of the Realm, High Admiral Karen, moved its paw in a gesture for the Guard admiral to take a seat and continue the conversation.

"High Admiral, in the performance of their duties my staff have had a certain Earth-born human male by the name of Teodor Korzeniowski under surveillance for some time. He and his Realm-born legal mate recently attended the Guard graduation ceremony on *Walpurg Station*. The one at which I believe you officiated."

"It was my privilege to introduce our Imperial Majesty to our fellow loyal Citizens. Please go on, Guard Admiral."

"While attending the graduation, the human Teodor made a number of comments in a tone our analysts understand to be mocking, cynical, perhaps even threatening. Many of these comments seem to be derived from, or relating to, events in recent Earth history. Our anthropologists have given their opinion as to the meaning of these comments, but as the High Admiral is widely recognized as an expert on matters pertaining to cultural and political events on planet Earth." He gave his superior a gesture of respect. "We were hoping ... I was hoping, you could find the time to put these comments into context."

"You have the data available now?" The High Admiral asked as it melted out of its quadrupedal shape and into a bipedal shape better suited for the tasks ahead. It pushed aside a stack of documents and made room in front of the interface. Then it got up and gestured to Guard Admiral Reinier—that he should walk around the desk and sit in front of the interface.

The High Admiral walked over and occupied a chair facing the only blank wall space in the room. The wall slid open revealing a screen.

"I'm sorry, Guard Admiral Reinier, I hope I am not too abrupt. But I know you're a busy officer with many responsibilities, so if you could present your evidence now, we can begin."

Guard Admiral Reinier was rather taken back. He wasn't quite prepared to go into details on the spot. He had thought it might take many days to get onto the High Admiral's calendar. Then, there was the High Admiral itself. He knew about the 'changing,' most higher ranking officers knew of it, but to see it in person was rather an unnerving experience. If the rumors he heard were true, it would only need a few drops of his blood[61] or a chunk of his flesh and the High Admiral could become him. Not the mind of course, but the body. A replica so complete that even the most sensitive instruments couldn't tell them apart. He sat at the interface and identifying himself to the computer began to retrieve his files.

"I'm sorry, High Admiral. I did not hope that you would find time for me so soon. It will only take a few moments to put the data together."

"Take your time, Guard Admiral. Can I get you something to eat or to drink?"

"Thank you, no." Guard Admiral Reinier replied as he made certain that the supplementary evidence was available if called for.

High Admiral Karen had gotten up and mixed several items together at a piece of furniture at the far end of the room. When it returned to its seat, Guard Admiral Reinier could see and smell that it was holding a transparent glass cylinder filled with ice, a clear mixture of vegetable products, alcohol and various alkaloids. It was far from appealing.

The High Admiral held up the glass, proudly showing it to Guard Admiral Reinier, "It's called a 'Gin and Tonic.' It is made from products acquired from the planet Earth." It looked admiringly at the glass and added, "Alcohol has little effect on thenardites, but I do so enjoy the taste of quinine and juniper berries. One of the few tastes that travels well between my various ... body shapes. It's interesting that when I'm a human the smell reminds me of home. In no other shape does it bring on that feeling. It still smells good, but no yearnings for home and hearth."

Guard Admiral Reinier was relieved to finally start the presentation. He was far from comfortable being in the presence of superior officers that were so high up [the food chain] that they could behave in so relaxed a manor with their juniors. High Admiral Karen moved effortlessly in society circles that he could only view through secured windows. Lunches with cabinet officials, amusements and sports with members of the Imperial family, even after dinner chats with the Imperial Majesty herself. No, Guard Admiral Reinier could hardly afford the time, let alone the danger of letting down his shields, to ever be as comfortable as the Commander in Chief, the High Admiral of the United Forces, the Protector of the Realm, Karen.

The first surveillance images appeared on the screen in front of the High Admiral. A computer generated voice read off time, place, and additional data pertinent to the subject's mental and emotional state.

{"13:07:46 station time, human male Teodor Korzeniowski is showing signs of apprehension. Recording: "Big crowd tonight. ... Hey, Thresher. I wonder how many of your old university buddies are here tonight?""}

{"13:07:53 station time, human female Thresher Korzeniowski is showing signs of excitement, with low levels of fear. Recording: "If the lights stay on I know one who didn't show up." Human male Teodor Korzeniowski is making sounds consistent with human amusement."}

The High Admiral turned and looked at Guard Admiral Reinier. "Your surveillance is quite good. You looked into this university reference?"

{Pausing playback}

"Yes, High Admiral. The humans are referring to an incident that occurred some years ago, when the human female Thresher, was at university studying medical technologies. One of her fellow dormmates shut off all the lights in the dorm building while attempting to deactivate the curfew monitoring systems. We have made inquires and find no evidence of any but youthful and amorous motives."

"Well, I guess we have all been there, Guard Admiral. Proceed."

Guard Admiral Reinier never had been there, but didn't make a habit of contradicting his superiors.

{"13:33:24 station time, human male Teodor Korzeniowski is showing signs of decreasing apprehension. Recording: "Will you look at those seats! Things are looking up. I know, when the jackals start their speeches, I'll lay down and catch up on some sleep. Wake me when the boss comes out and they start the book burning.""}

{"13:33:28 station time, human female Thresher Korzeniowski is showing signs of agitation, possibly mild anger. Recording: "Teodor! Don't be a *kripslod*!""}

{Pausing playback}

"The anthropologists feel that the male human is showing disrespect for Realm authority and that the female either fears detection or disagrees with his attitude. Additionally we know that 'jackals' refers to a carnivorous mammalian animal native to planet Earth.

"The term 'boss' is used to designate a person having authority. The male's voice patterns would seem to indicate that he finds it disagreeable that this individual is in this position of authority. Since this reference to a 'boss' is linked to the term 'book burning' and that no such actions were undertaken during the ceremonies, we have little solid evidence to reach a conclusion as to who this 'boss' person is.

"As to the term, 'book burning' it seems to be in reference to politically or religiously motivated destruction of documents expressing beliefs out of harmony with the beliefs of those initiating the conflagration. Again our anthropologists suggest this is a remark intended to express the male's misguided belief that the government of the Realm represses dissident ideas."

"Very good, Guard Admiral. I believe your experts have hit upon our human friend's ideology, exactly. The jackal is traditionally thought of as a scavenger of more powerful predator's kills. I think it would be a reasonable conclusion to explain our human's euphemisms thus: "when the jackals start their speeches" meaning the speeches he imagined we underlings would deliver prior to introducing the "boss," our Imperial Majesty, who would then lead her followers in a sacrifice to twice blessed intolerance and xenophobia."

"The [bastard!][62]... I'm sorry, High Admiral, but trash like this has no place in the Realm."

"Your loyalty to our Imperial Majesty is a great virtue, Guard Admiral Reinier, but we must remember always that we are professionals. We must keep a calm spleen if we are to prove useful to those we loyally serve. I have yet to hear any call to action on the human's part, perhaps it would be best if we continue." Karen spoke in almost a purr.

{"13:53:17 station time, human male Teodor Korzeniowski is showing signs of mild tension, perhaps related to humor, or personal safety. Recording: "Thresher? With palagonites which comes first, a switch over to solid food or the knowledge that society frowns on you eating your fellow Citizens no matter how tasty they look?" ... "Never mind

problem solved." Continuing: "Would make a nice picture for a [Mother's Day] [card.]""}
{Pausing playback}
"There was no response picked up from his mate. We concluded the forgoing speech was a harmless observation about a palagonite hatchling seated with its mother in the row behind the suspects—"

Karen looked at him. "Not good enough." it whispered.

"I am truly sorry, High Admiral. In retrospect it was possible that some danger to the Citizenry was presented by the suspect at this time. A full review of our surveillance of Earth-born humans will be undertaken by my staff immediately!"

"Thank you, Guard Admiral. It is a difficult course we travel. We can not know what goes through the mind of every Citizen or visitor. If we underestimate dangers, we risk lives. If we overestimate, we risk public support. Personally, I still have not seen any evidence that these humans pose any danger, but we learn. We learn. Please, continue."

{"13:79:39 station time, human male Teodor Korzeniowski is showing signs of rising interest in the proceedings. Recording: Thresher? Your dad was in the Fleet, what's up with those formations? I thought troops marched in straight rows, not all spread out like that.""}

{"13:79:41 station time, palagonite male, subject not currently under surveillance. No authorization for detailed record search at this time." Recording: "Human. It would be difficult for a military formation made up of Citizens of so widely varying sizes to march in rows. That's only done planetside when the formation only has members belonging to a single species. The more common formation, the one that you're watching tonight, is called a Crystal Formation. ... My old drill instructor, Fleet Junior Chief Crewperson Drusus told us that it was like a zinc oxide crystal, big and small atoms joined together to make a uniform structure. He always had a way of explaining things. ... If you have any questions, just ask me—spent forty-three years in the Fleet. ..." Recording stopped at this point because non authorized subject has disengaged conversation with subject under surveillance."}

{"13:80:26 station time, human male Teodor Korzeniowski is showing signs of anxiety. Recording: "Thanks for the information! ... Citizen.""}

{"14:36:19 station time, human male Teodor Korzeniowski is showing signs of intense emotional activity. Could be anger, anxiety, confusion or a combination. Warning: subject assuming standing position! Normal Condition. The Imperial Majesty is entering the stadium. Recording: "Black uniforms, torches and flower bearers? Who wrote this crap?""}

{"14:37:61 station time, Warning: subject human male Teodor Korzeniowski has resumed seated position at an unexpected time!"}

"Anxiety, anger, And confusion? Your emotion deciphering equipment seems to be having a little difficulty analyzing this subject. What activity was in progress when Teodor made that last statement?"

{Pausing playback}

"You had just saluted our Imperial Majesty. Then let's see, ... our Imperial Majesty was acknowledging the crowds show of respect. ... Yes, here on the screen: The eleven children bringing the flowers up to our Imperial Majesty. They had just started down the walkways. Problem?"

"I'm just a bit sensitive to criticism. I tried very hard to arrange for a solemn and emotionally uplifting ceremony that evening. ... Additionally, I have found that many of our higher ranking Fleet and Guard officers enjoy living the good life. They do look so much better under dim light conditions.

"Well, perhaps he's right. Certainly not crap, but I do have to agree with the human—[a little over the top] with the children. Sometimes one is tempted to use anti-matter to grit the path. You can skip ahead, Guard Admiral. He is just making further references to my clueless theatrics."

"High Admiral, *you* were responsible for such a moving graduation ceremony? You must never sleep, being concerned with so many responsibilities."

"Please, Guard Admiral, there is no need to lick my ears. Not that I don't enjoy it. I do. But there is no need. Honestly, you have no idea if the graduation was moving or not, as your many responsibilities kept you from attending. We are both just simple servants of our Imperial Majesty. We do as we are assigned. ... When I was newly promoted a Guard captain and sent here to Guard Operations Center-Palagon, I was put on a committee assigned to modernize the Guard. We created new uniforms, simplified protocol, and made new arraignments for ceremonies like this recent graduation. The committee is long disbanded, but as High Admiral, I still like to keep my paws on the kill. ... Please, continue, Guard Admiral Reinier."

{14:42:15 station time, human male Teodor—"}

{Pausing playback}

"This section drifts somewhat. We only had authorization to record some of the participants and not others. Briefly, the palagonite mother sitting behind Teodor was concerned about his—Teodor Korzeniowski's—health. Most probably because he sat down so unexpectedly. The humans explained that nothing was wrong, ... words, words, words, then, this part is interesting.

{"14:50:83 station time, human female Thresher Korzeniowski is showing signs of mild annoyance. Recording: "See! I told you they were gentle beings. Keep this in mind the next time you think they just want to put us out on hunting reserves, or any of that other crap you always worry about. I'm sorry Teodor. I'm just not used to standing out at public events. Will—You—Please, ... just sit there quietly.""}

{Pausing playback}

"We have a copy of a past medical examination of one, Teodor Korzeniowski. During the examination, he made statements that led the initiating technician to conclude that the patient believed the palagonites to be a threat to him, personally. The med tech on duty watch at the time was one, Thresher Selverlinck. Later, his legal mate, Thresher Korzeniowski. She recorded in the day log that the initiating technician may have misunderstood the description given by Teodor Korzeniowski of an accidental collision he had with a palagonite male a few days previous. It would seem our suspect does not trust palagonites. That could explain his irrational dislike for our Imperial Majesty. Unless the human female suspected she was under observation her correction of her mate's distorted reasoning could show she is not in agreement with his subversive behavior."

"If that's the case, Guard Admiral, she should have informed the proper authorities of his mental illness right away."

"True! When will the Citizens learn they can't just ignore ailing family members. They need to be isolated and treated, not tolerated. ... Thank you, High Admiral, for your invaluable help. I'll have the suspects brought in for more detailed examination."

"Guard Admiral? Nothing else was said at the graduation?"

"A little more, but I have taken too much of your time already."

"Guard Admiral Reinier, please, continue with your report."

{"14:77:03 station time, human male Teodor Korzeniowski is showing signs of general calmness. Recording: "Who is that officer standing next to the Imperial Majesty? I've never seen anything like it."""}

{"14:77:26 station time, human female Thresher Korzeniowski is showing signs of general calmness, perhaps a readiness to enter sleep. Recording: "It's a thenardite, probably Guard Admiral Wilymia Alphrontex, but I can't be sure. I've never seen a rank insignia like that."""}

"Would you pause that please, Guard Admiral Reinier."

"With pleasure, High Admiral!"

{Pausing playback}

"The female mentioned my parent. They are acquainted?"

"My department contacted retired Guard Admiral Wilymia Alphrontex. She remembers that she gave a lecture on the history of medical ethics at several medical schools during the years that Thresher Selverlinck was attending university. Your mother concluded that she could have been the only thenardite the young human has ever had contact with and that owing to your close family resemblance, it would be reasonable for Thresher to mistake the daughter for the mother."

"Very reasonable. My parent always is. Guard Admiral, just a note about grammar. Not of great importance, but still. When referring to any thenardite the proper pronoun is *it*, not *she* and not *he*. Just a little something for you to place in the back of your mind."

"I'm sorry, High Admiral. I meant no offense. Your mother, ... correction, your parent, referred to you as a female offspring. Just so I don't inadvertently—"

Karen interrupted. "If you cut wood thin enough you can see light through it. There is no need to dissect the language until we have only cells in the dish. If you can remember to, and it causes no undue distress, please refer to me in a genderless way. If you forget, well, it is of no real importance anyway. Are there still additional recordings?"

"Yes, High Admiral."

{"14:78:01 station time, human male Teodor Korzeniowski

is showing signs of increased excitement perhaps humor." Recording: "No wonder they're dying out. Who would want to mate with that!""}

"*Verdammt nochmal!*"[63] the High Admiral roared as it jumped to its feet.

Before hearing *its* statement about genders, Guard Admiral Reinier had been dreading his superior's reaction to the human's slur, but since the High Admiral implied that mating was not a thenardite function, he had let his shields down. Not a wise move. 'Hull breach, decks five through eleven!'

"I'm sorry, High Admiral. The human's conduct is inexcusable!" He thoughtfully avoided reminding the Commander in Chief of its earlier comments about keeping a cool spleen and professionalism. A stupid comment like that and years of hard work would be jettisoned away. He forgot to pause the playback.

{"15:00:05 station time, the human female is showing signs of intense emotional distress."}

{"15:01:42 station time, palagonite female, subject not currently under surveillance. No authorization for detailed record search at this time. Recording: "Someone close?""}

{"15:02:16 station time, human male Teodor Korzeniowski is showing signs of increased emotional activity. Recording: "I'm not certain, but I think her father received a medal like that after her mother died.""}

{"15:02:72 station time, palagonite female, subject not currently under surveillance. No authorization for detailed record search at this time. Recording: "Dear one, you're not alone. We're all family.""}

{"15:03:33 station time, Warning: human female, Thresher Korzeniowski, has risen and is making physical contact with palagonite female that was just speaking to her. Correction: no danger. Physical contact consisted of activity interpreted as affectionate—between two female Citizens in a state of high emotion. Recording not resumed at this point because non authorized subject has disengaged conversation with subject under surveillance"}

"Stop the playback!" The High Admiral commanded. Then returning to its usual quite and calm way of speaking, "I'm sorry, Guard Admiral Reinier. I did not mean to shout at you. What was that about the female human and a medal?"

"The records indicate that Thresher Korzeniowski is the offspring of a legally mated pair. Father: Carsteloot Selverlinck, now a retired Fleet chief crewperson living on Phenak. Mother: Sanne Selverlinck, formerly a Fleet chief crewperson of engineering, killed while on active duty aboard an APV—the TFSS *Skyfish*.

"Our Imperial Majesty awarded Carsteloot and Thresher the *Realm Medal of Family Sacrifice* thirty-four years ago. We have not been granted permission to fully investigate retired Fleet Chief Crewperson Carsteloot Selverlinck at this time."

"How did Sanne Selverlinck die?"

"The commanding officer of the *Skyfish* reported that a fire had broken out in the main engineering section. It spread rapidly and did not respond to any containment methods.

"There were thirty-two Citizens in the section at the time. At least nine were killed within the first few moments of the fire and the rest were cut off from both the exits and the personal protection devices. Fleet Chief Crewperson of Engineering Sanne Selverlinck was in command of the main engineering section at the time.

"She became aware that the fire could not be contained and that the ship was in imminent danger of destruction. She used the emergency airlock override [keys] and evacuated the section. The fire was extinguished. All thirty-two Citizens, including Sanne Selverlinck, died either as a direct result of the fire or from sudden catastrophic exposure to the vacuum of space.

"Fleet Chief Crewperson of Engineering Sanne Selverlinck was posthumously awarded the *Fleet Medal of Bravery* and her family were awarded, as I previously stated, the *Realm Medal of Family Sacrifice.*"

"Do we have any record of how the family reacted?"

"I think I know where you're going, High Admiral and I'm happy to report that my department already made an investigation. Fleet Chief Crewperson Carsteloot Selverlinck remained on the active service list for another twenty-three years. Here is a list of his performance reviews and the commendations he received. No indications that he was ever other than a loyal and competent member of the Fleet.

"Thresher was about five years old at the time of her mother's death. According to records at the Office of the Imperial Majesty, our Imperial Majesty, as is still the custom, personally presented the medal to Carsteloot and gave the human child a hands only hug around the shoulders. Some kind words were spoken and finished her attention to Thresher by licking her face. The child is reported to have told our Imperial Majesty that she loved her and then burst into tears. She was still crying when her father took her back to their lodgings.

"I ordered a team to discreetly enter the temporary rental unit the human couple now inhabit and verified that Thresher Selverlinck ... that is, Thresher Korzeniowski, still retains the medal in a box of ornaments and valuables."

"It would seem she harbors no ill will for the Fleet or for the person of our Imperial Majesty."

"Our researchers came to that same conclusion, High Admiral."

"So, Guard Admiral Reinier, what do we do about this *kripslod* and his loyal mate? Remember, no [martyrs!]"

"That reminds me, High Admiral. One of my top investigators ... that is former investigators, had an interesting comment about this case. He said, "Teodor often criticizes the security services for what he sees as overly harsh and oppressive behavior. Please don't let him be right.""

"It would seem you had a philosopher in your midst, Guard Admiral Reinier. You had him reässigned?"

"It would not be prudent to trust the safety of the Realm to those who exhibit too much sentimentality. He will spend the remaining days of his commission assigned as the political officer on a government funded mining station in the Wolnyn System. Out of the way, but still useful."

"Is sentimentality the only reason? Could it also involve the close contacts between one of the subjects of your investigation and the Guard captain's daughter, Medical Officer Guard First Lieutenant Frida. I presented her with her dagger several years ago. As I said before, Guard Admiral Reinier, I like to keep my paws on the kill. I knew about your investigation within hours of your opening Frida's file."

"Medical Officer Guard First Lieutenant Frida speaks very highly of her old school friend Thresher, but what about *our* dear friend Teodor? We need to find a way to make him show us where *his* friendship is truly directed."

"Perfect, that will work, Guard Admiral. Teodor professes to love his mate. If he is a dedicated agent of the Clinohumites he would certainly be willing to risk all, even his mate, Thresher, to get his hands on military equipment invaluable to their terrorist activities. Let us give him a chance to pick sides. If he chooses Thresher over the Clinohumites, then he becomes little more than a nuisance to us. On the other hand, if he sides with them ... Well, he is mortal and accidents happen every day—especially on a mining outpost.

"Check the status of the RealmRock mine in the Wolnyn System. I think you'll find that the little piece of paradise you marooned Guard Captain Evert on is scheduled soon for deäctivation. Electromagnetic conditions make it inaccessible for strictly automated exploitation and geological instabilities have already cost the lives of forty-nine Citizens. It is a death trap and a [hell hole], but that hasn't stopped the Department of Strategic Materials from planning to send several Xz-7 planetoid mining torpedoes to the site. Hope is ever reconditioned in the minds of our Realm's ministers. But eventually, even they must bow to public opinion."

"The mine will begin shutdown procedures within forty-eight days, High Admiral. It would seem that Guard Captain Evert will be coming home sooner than I thought."

"He's a fine officer and I was not in agreement with your evaluation of his effectiveness. He was coming home soon anyway. When this mission is completed I may have him reässigned to my staff. Who knows, he may retire long after you do, Guard Admiral Reinier."

"I am rightfully chastised, High Admiral. My only hope is to be allowed to bask in your wisdom for years to come. I hope you agree, Excellency."

"I agree. You are very good at your job, Guard Admiral Reinier. ... See! We do learn. Both of us. Now, if you were a Clinohumite terrorist, what would you do for a Xz-7?"

"Anything it took to get my hands on one. They're small and relatively easy to transport. Using it against an inhabited planet I could kill millions. They are well guarded, I trust."

"Until they're ready to be used, they are kept on a Fleet warship under heavy security. Two Guard ships are also kept close by at all times. ... But a mining station with casualties as high as this one has is always in need of med techs. If you travel with your med tech mate you have access to the site. Access to the site means you're in position anytime the torpedoes are moved. A little [*léger de main*] and you have at least one of these superb agents of death for your very own. The one down side is that with the need to pull injured miners out of the mine tunnels so often, your mate stands a very high chance of getting maimed or killed soon after she arrives. A small sacrifice perhaps. The pay is not unreasonable and RealmRock will cover relocating expenses.

"Let's put out the word and see if we can get them interested. Make it subtle. Overplay this and we give away our motives. As the Earth humans of *Deutsch-Ostafrika* would say, 'Haraka, haraka haina baraka.' That is to say, 'Hurry, hurry gets you nowhere.' We have time to do it right, Guard Admiral Reinier, but only one chance."

High Admiral Karen got up from its chair and walked over to one of those strange mechanical devices that seemed to be perched atop every piece of furniture in the room. Over this particular device hung a portrait of a human male in half profile. He looked to be elderly—at least that was what the facial features and fur color led the Guard Admiral to conclude. What brought it so clearly to Reinier's attention was the subject's rather serious countenance contrasted by the flamboyant fur profusely perched atop his upper lip and the ridiculously ornate hat or helmet with the spike sticking out of its top that he was wearing.

The High Admiral [wound-up] one of the devices and made some adjustments to its mechanism. Then it looked through some flat objects on a shelf below it. Selecting one and removing it from its [paper] sleeve, it attached it to the upper surface of the device. Turning back to face the Guard admiral it continued, "This will be your assignment and I have the fullest confidence in your ability to carry it to a worthwhile conclusion, Guard Admiral Reinier, but if you need something from me—please, you have only to ask."

Guard Admiral Reinier was relived to understand the meeting was now over, "Thank you, High Admiral, it is an honor to serve. I will let you know if I require anything from you." He stood and saluted. "Our Imperial Majesty!"

"Our Imperial Majesty. *Auf Wiedersehen,* Guard Admiral Reinier. Until we meet again. "

Guard Admiral Reinier left the Protector of the Realm's office and lingered in the outer office just long enough to put on his water repellent over-coat. The randomness of planetside weather was one of the reasons he was very glad to have his department housed comfortably on a station.

As he passed through the door into the corridor he could just make out more music coming from High Admiral Karen's office.

"Un bel dì, vedremo
levarsi un fil di fumo Sull'estremo
confin del mare
E poi la nave appare
E poi la nave è bianca." [...]
[-*Un bel dì* from *Madama Butterfly* by Giacomo Puccini[64]]

He thought to himself, "All that senseless clutter! And music! Playing music in your office and while on duty! That is certainly an odd individual. Still another good reason to remain in space. Not a bad idea to keep a safe distance from one's superiors."

The music faded into comfortable nothingness as he closed the door and hurried to shuttle back to *Aegerite Station*.

Chapter Fourteen
A Test of Loyalties

Some insignificant station out in the Realm

Teodor Korzeniowski felt like a true *kripslod*. It had taken him two years to figure it out, but at last he did. It wasn't his mate's gender, it wasn't her lack of connections, it wasn't her education, her age, her intelligence, or her work ethic. It was he that kept her from getting a good job. He finally figured it out with help from his father-in-law.

Thresher's father was retired Fleet Chief Crewperson Carsteloot Selverlinck and the retired Fleet chief crewperson loved his little girl very much. The retired Fleet chief crewperson tolerated Teodor—but perhaps tolerated is too strong a word for how he felt. It might be better to say that he acknowledged, that in this ever expanding universe,[65] there existed a human male called by his parents Teodor Korzeniowski. What he never seemed to acknowledge was that, through some terrible injustice, his wonderful daughter, the pride of his life, his little jewel, and this... person, Teodor Korzeniowski, were a legally mated pair.

When he communicated in from his home on Phenak, he always asked for Thresher and if she wasn't at home, "Then I'll communicate with her later." If he sent her something RSDS he would address it simply, "to Thresher Selverlinck." Teodor was certain that if it wasn't for the fact that his father-in-law religiously watched etiquette and protocol programs daily on the screens, he would have by now sent an RSDS package addressed to: "Thresher c/o that no good low life bum, Teodor Korzeniowski."

No, Carsteloot Selverlinck was not happy with his daughter's choice of a mate. "Even Fuzzi Eck'crawd managed to find a mate that worked for a living and she was never the brightest indicator light on the control panel."

So, you can imagine Teodor's surprise, when one day, the Fleet chief crewperson communicated in and asked for Thresher and when told she was out, said, {"That's good, Teodor. I want to talk to you."}

Teodor was quite taken back. He didn't know what to say. Literally, he didn't know how to address his father-in-law. Up to that moment, he never had to. His mind raced. Should he call him: Dad? Citizen Selverlinck? Retired Fleet Chief Crewperson Carsteloot Selverlinck? Finally, in near desperation, he hit on it: "Chief,[66] it's truly a pleasure to hear from you. Is everything going well?"

{"Teodor, what in blazes! What stupid stunts are you up to now! Do you have any idea what your thoughtless actions are doing to Thresher? ... No, you don't! I just talked to an old shipmate of mine on *Walpurg*. You disloyal *kripslod*! You have lighted up her security clearance, burned so many holes in it that it ... it couldn't hold ixiolite[67] half buried in the surface of a failed star.

{"Retired Fleet Junior Chief Crewperson Passchyer told me, Thresher, my perfect little jewel, doesn't have the security clearance to [render offal]! And we both know it's all because of you!

{"Now, here's the deal. There's an opening for a med tech on a dismal little planetoid mine out in the Wolnyn System. It's run by RealmRock with some major subsidies from the Realm Department of Strategic Materials. Are you following me? Right! Retired Fleet Junior Chief Crewperson Passchyer, bless him, helped put a deal through with a Black Tunic named Evert. You might remember that Evert's daughter was at university with Thresher. Well, Evert's the political officer out at that mine site.

{"Here's were you come in. Guard Captain Evert put his pension on the line and convinced his superiors to get Thresher a chance to prove herself to the bosses down at

RealmRock. If they approve — and you better hope they do — then she gets a six-month tour of duty, and maybe, just maybe, when it's over, she gets her hard earned reputation back.

{"I'm sending you two the funds to get over to RealmRock *Dorallchar Station* by the 19th. You breech this opportunity for Thresher and I'll open you up fore to aft. Understand, Korzeniowski?"}

"Yes, Chief!"

{"Good! I'm glad we understand each other. Say hello to Thresher for me. And tell her, "Daddy loves her." That is all! This communication ends now."}

* * *

Dorallchar Station, the Realm

Seven days later, Teodor sat in the reception area of RealmRock's offices, contemplating, "It's funny, at a time when the people of Earth were looking at fire and thinking, 'What a great idea!' the inhabitants of the Empire of the Palagonites possessed faster-than-light star ships. Still, thousands of years later, they leave printed brochures in waiting rooms so bored Citizens have something to read."

Teodor shuffled though the brochures hoping to find something to take his mind off of Thresher's ordeal. He finally picked up one that seemed to relate to something he had heard about earlier. A few hours before, while he and Thresher were eating down deck in the company cafeteria, Teodor overheard some company employees discussing a new mining technology and here it was in glorious four color printing — the Xz-7 torpedo.

"A better Realm achieved by smashing planets into powder." he sarcastically thought and then shuddered at the disturbing thoughts racing though his mind. "Asbestos insulation, thalidomide, radium coated indicator dials, mercury carroting, lead surface coatings. I just hope the Realm tests out its *wunder* products better than the people of Earth ever do.

Teodor looked up and again noticed the reception team sitting behind a low partition. One was an ettringite and the other was a halotrichite. The halotrichite was the greeter and shower. As the various Citizens entered from the hallway she would greet them and when they were called for, she would show them the way to their appointment. The ettringite never greeted anyone. She just worked at the interface.

He returned the brochure to the pile. The ettringite was looking at him. He looked at her. The interface urgently called for her attention. A short time later, Thresher came out into the reception area.

Teodor thought his mate looked all done in. "Was it rough in there? You looked wiped." he whispered to her, then he gave her a shoulder hug and called her their little pet name, "*Liebchen!*"

"I got the job." she said, almost crying.

"I can see you're very happy about it. Maybe we should go somewhere private and talk."

"Can we? Please!"

She dropped off their visitor passes with security and they exited out into the public area.

"Crap! The one good paying job I get and I don't want it. Teodor, it's horrible! It's Realm funded so they had to show me the safety reports. In the last three years since they opened the mine, there have been fifty-three miners killed and over a hundred seventy seriously injured. They're trying to find new ways to extract the minerals safely, but for the moment, it's still strictly hands on. Hands on? Just a few days ago a med tech was nearly burned to death trying to help an injured miner. It's the year 1758 [fTF] and he was burned by boiling rock! Oh, Teodor, what am I going to do?

Dad worked so hard getting me this interview and ... you don't know this, but he has spent so much of his savings helping us pay our bills." Thresher sat down—nearly collapsed—onto a bench and sobbed.

"Thresher, you don't have to take the job. I don't want you to and I know your dad feels the same way. He would never want to see his 'perfect little jewel' put in that kind of danger."

Thresher looked up at her mate, "He always called me that when I was growing up. How did you know?"

"He used that expression on the phone. I mean, when he communicated in the other day. And I had a pretty good guess about how we were stabilizing our orbit as well. My, how the Chief can get a point across!"

"Daddy yelled at you?"

"He was ... forceful. He told me about your security clearance. It's my stupid big mouth, isn't it?"

"You're not stupid. You just don't understand—" Then noticing the security agent approaching them across the path, she spoke up, "It's all right, Citizen. Just a little disappointment. With the help of my mate here, I'll get over it."

"Citizens." the security agent said as she continued on her way across the public area.

"Perfect timing. That's what I need to honestly talk to you about. I should have explained it to you when we first met, but I thought you knew it yourself ... don't you see? I've known it since I was a child, it's a fact of life.

"My dear intelligent, but inexperienced, mate. We are never alone. We are always being monitored. You just have to get used to it. When we're walking in the park, the [arcade], any public place, there is always something or someone listening. Most of the time it's a computer and they don't care if it's amorous whispering or shouting about the big game. All they care about is how you feel when you say it. Remember that examination room?—When I treated your kidney? It didn't know if behemoth was a obscenity, but it did know what emotions you were feeling when you shouted it at the top of your lungs. That's how the surveillance works. If you say or do something that perks up the computer's interest, then it hands you off to a living breathing sapient[68] being for closer study. That's why you keep getting us into trouble. It's not that you mean anything by it, but you keep pulling the pressure alarm when there is no decompression! You don't have to be a mindless automaton, but you do have to use common sense—"

"Thresher, I'm so very sorry. I did know it. I just didn't want to care about it. I had to show off. I had to be the [big shot rebel,] and I caused you to lose years of your life. I hurt your dad too. Please, don't take that job. You'll ... No! We'll think of something. [If I keep my nose clean] will they reset your clearance—like with a credit account?"

"I think you get reëvaluated every time you apply for a position in Federal Territory. ... That's it! Let's just keep out of sensor range for a year or two and then I'll put in an application for something—anything—on say *Walpurg Station* and see if we're forgiven."

"I know talk is cheap, but whatever I can do, I'll do it. We'll get by and we'll stay together, *Liebchen*. Whatever happens, we have got to find away to pay the Chief back.

In the offices of RealmRock, another Citizen had been shown where to proceed for a meeting with one of the many mid-level managers whose offices line the hallway stretching outward from the reception area. Behind the low partition, the ettringite looked up from the interface and over towards her now returning halotrichite companion and stated philosophically, "Talk is rarely cheap. In fact, sometimes, it can cost you a great deal."

Chapter Fifteen
The Wolnyn System

Guard Operations Center-Palagon
Planet Palagon, Proculus System, the Realm

"Ach, wie ist's möglich dann,
Daß ich dich lassen kann;
Hab' dich von Herzen lieb,
Das glaube mir! [...]"
-*Treue Liebe* [Thuringian Folk Song/Friedrich Wilhelm Kücken][69]

The music drifted out of the Protector of the Realm's office when the aide put her head in to request permission to send in Fleet Second Ensign Agricola[70] with an important dispatch from Fleet High Admiral Maximinus.

Fleet Second Ensign Agricola was a rather worried palagonite. He had never met the Protector of the Realm before. It was just that he had been in the wrong place at exactly the wrong time and now found out that there was a significant price to pay for being noticed by your superiors.

Fleet High Admiral Maximinus and Fleet Senior Captain Critolaus had been studying a report on the screens when the young Fleet second ensign walked into the conference room. Two hours before, Agricola had been attending a training lecture in that same room and had inadvertently left his notes on a chair. Now, "He was just the fine young officer they needed to convey a situation report to the Protector of the Realm. First however, they would all need to stop by the office of the political officer and have a little friendly talk about secrecy and treason."

Now, some sixty or seventy minutes later, Agricola was shown into the office of the Protector of the Realm.

"Our Imperial Majesty!"

"Our Imperial Majesty. Good day, Fleet Second Ensign Agricola. If you have been permitted the time ... please take a seat." The High Admiral said while pointing to a palagonite bench-seat.

"Thank you, sir. " he replied and then noticing the decor he added, "This room is wonderful!" dropping his report sack and gesturing with both arms.

"I'm glad you like it." the Protector of the Realm responded, rather taken back by the young males exuberance. "I hope that there was nothing breakable?" it asked, pointing down to the report sack now laying in a heap on the floor.

"Oh no, sir. Just some notes and a portable interface, ... Is that a mechanical recording seismograph over there? It looks lanarkite. It must be really old!"

"Actually, it's a recording barograph and it's Earth made, *Englisch* I think. [One of my parents] bought it in London many years ago. ... I assume that you've been sent here to give me the information I requested about the Xz-7's that were to have been supplied to RealmRock?"

"I'm sorry, sir. I guess I should get right to the point. Fleet High Admiral Maximinus wanted to keep you informed of how things in the Wolnyn System are going. He said this is just preliminary and that when additional facts come in he'll communicate in with you right away."

"And why were you sent, Fleet Second Ensign Agricola, and not Fleet Senior Captain Critolaus?"

The Fleet Second Ensign never got the chance to answer the Protector of the Realm's question, because just then, Karen's aide rushed in and interrupted, "Excellency! Fleet High Admiral Maximinus is communicating in. He needs to speak with you about a most urgent matter! On two."

"Thank you, Sonja. ... Max, what's the problem? I have your Fleet second ensign here—"

{"High Admiral Karen, one of our Xz-7's is missing!"}

Chapter Sixteen
Catalyst

Idocrase System, the Realm

Idocrase System is a dismal little [backwater] in the Realm's Fourth Octant. It consists of an unremarkable star, the scattered remains of one or more still-born rocky planets, two ice giants, and three gas giants—one large enough to possibly be taken for a failed star. There are no planets or natural satellites capable of being inhabited by Citizen's of the Realm, without considerable technological assistance. The system does contain a number of synthetic structures, but few of those remain operational. Included among the unused and derelict edifices are a long decommissioned Imperial Fleet ship-breaking complex and hundreds of stations and facilities also dating from the time of the Empire of the Palagonites. One of only a few modern constructions still possessing life-support in this system is the joint Realm-private venture called *Idocrase Station Four*.

The Idocrase System is rarely visited, as repeated system-wide surveys have failed to discover commercially viable concentrations of strategic materials and there is little there to interest the researcher or the tourist. It is however, the location where several of the better known commercial transport firms dump their obsolete, irreparably damaged and redundant spacecraft.

Idocrase Ship Brokering and Salvage Company has its headquarters on *Idocrase Station Four* and is the area's largest employer. Using mostly robotics, they store, maintain, and render into reüsable parts, the tens of thousands of old ships left in their charge. They also, with Fleet assistance, protect this strategically and financially valuable waste from the pirates and scavengers that are always prowling about in the lesser traveled areas of the Realm.

The Idocrase Ship Brokering and Salvage Company has an interesting, if little publicized, history. After the Empire of the Palagonites collapsed into civil war and was resurrected as *The Thenardite Brokered Federation of Planetary Republics and Political Bodies*, something needed to be done quickly with those humans who had, to a lesser or to a greater extent, helped their ettringite owners in carrying out the extermination of their fellow humans. On one end of the spectrum of 'tainted' humans were the simple house slaves who had continued faithfully performing menial duties in the hope of survival for themselves and their families. On the other end were those humans who had used the massacre of the human race for their own selfish purposes. The humans with the whips, the full bellies, and the private agendas, who drove the starving human slave labors to eventual death.

The solution of what to do with these 'tainted' humans was to be found in the Idocrase System, or more specifically, in the offices, housing complexes, support centers, and workshops, of Idocrase Ship Brokering and Salvage Company. The 'tainted' humans were simply shipped off to provide labor at the newly created and Realm subsidized company.

After the civil war had ended, a company that could collect and process the mechanical carcasses, both military and civilian, that now lay strewn across the Galaxy into something useful, was very much in demand. So the Idocrase Ship Brokering and Salvage Company prospered. The 'tainted' humans were provided for, put to work, and most importantly, kept out of public view. 'Problem solved!'

Today, the Idocrase Ship Brokering and Salvage Company is the third oldest continually operating company in the Realm and one of the the most profitable. It is privately run by the same human family that has had an interest in the company for over seventeen hundred years. It employs over fourteen thousand, mostly human, Citizens; many of whom are descendants of those who were associated with the company from the very beginning.

The Idocrase System is also home to a moderate sized medical facility called Kiezlyne Realmcare Clinic-Idocrase Station Four. This clinic is a wholly owned and highly profitable subsidiary of the Idocrase Ship Brokering and Salvage Company.

Cerdic-Three, the Realm

Teodor returned home to find his mate sitting in the small kitchen of the efficiency apartment they had rented on Cerdic-Three, with the near certainty that Thresher had been accepted for a job at Crindon Agri.

He was in an exceptionally playful mood, but Thresher was not. No, she sat with her face buried in her hands and sobbed like her world had just ended. In a way it had. Her dad had plunged deeper into his life-savings and had helped them to travel out here to Cerdic-Three, and now, this had happened! She had arrived at what she had been told was just to be a token interview—a mere formality. Crindon Agri had recently been awarded a contract to provide food products for the Fleet and their subsequent plans for expansion would necessitate larger medical facilities for all the additional workers to be added here on Cerdic-Three and at other locations around the Realm. The interview began and all indications were that she would soon find herself with long-term employment. Thresher had the necessary qualifications; she was legally mated and that gave her life the look of stability, and although her mate, Teodor, did have a few [demerits] on his record, her overall employment/credit/security record was adequate for the needs of the job description.

Half an hour into the interview and everything changed. With no warning, something on the interviewer's interface must have been abruptly altered and not for the better. The interviewer quickly regained his composure and apologizing to Thresher, asked her to return to the waiting room and give him time to make a few simple inquiries. An hour later the interviewer came out of his office and informed Thresher that, due to unforeseen circumstances, her employment would not be required at this time. Two armed security agents politely but firmly escorted her out of the building.

Overwhelmed by what had just happened, Thresher had wandered around the station's public areas for an hour or so before finally going back to the apartment. Then, she suffered the next blow. The management of the apartment building had a sudden change of thought and after giving her back some of what she had already paid them, informed her she and her mate would have twenty-five hours to vacate the premises.

Seeing Thresher in this state greatly affected Teodor. And as usual, he misdirected his anger and cursed the unfairness and corruption of whole damn Realm and its petty and [ugly as sin] dictator.

He was just in the midst of making matters worse by loudly proclaiming all the spleen-less and criminal character traits that he imagined the Imperial Majesty possessed, when someone approached their door and indicated a desire to communicate with them.

Teodor opened the door to find the lanarkite female that lived in the unit two doors down. He remembered her because she had been so kind and helpful when they moved in three days before. For the life of him he couldn't remember her name so he merely addressed her as ma'am (He laughed at the term Citizen in the best of times and today he positively hated the thought of it) and he asked her what he could do for her.

"Good day, Citizen. I'm sorry to disturb you in what is obviously a very difficult time, but I did want to let you know your voice can be clearly heard out in the common area. Not to be a busy-body, but one does need to be careful *who* they complain about, especially, in the hearing of others."

Thresher came up besides her mate and wisely took over the conversation with their conscientious neighbor, "I'm so sorry, Citizen Genovefa, if we disturbed you. As you know we just moved so I could take a position with Crindon Agri. Well, the job fell through and now it looks like we'll need to move again. It gets so tiring moving like this. Again, I'm sorry. My mate is just so concerned for my well being … Well, he wasn't thinking clearly and just overreacted. I hope what he said didn't cause you any harm." She looked sideways at Teodor and added, "He just needs to remember to take the time to think things through before he foolishly assigns blame for all the hardships in the universe."

The lanarkite gave an understanding gesture and explained, "As my little nephew likes to say, "Speak in haste, repent in solitary." He's in the Guard, you know. Anyway, I wasn't harmed by your mate's outburst. Offended, but not harmed. None of us is perfect, so I shouldn't wonder that we all say things we don't really mean. Now that I've reminded you of your duties as Citizens, I hope I can brighten your otherwise dimly-lit day. You see, I was sitting in my room thinking of what I could do to stop your mate from saying all those awful things about our most beloved Imperial Majesty and I thought of my little nephew. Actually, I thought of his father. That's my brother-in-law Fionnalagh and he works for a job placement firm on Phenak. To make the story short—I communicated with him and he had this job for a med tech just sitting in his files. You see, they've had trouble finding Citizens that want to move all the way out to Idocrase. I Guess it's a [little off the beaten track,] and it seems the local young people go off to university and never bother moving back. We've never had that trouble here, but I guess some places are like that. Anyway, to make the story short—here is the information he gave me. I hope it works out for you, you did seem to be such nice Citizens.

Thresher was again overwhelmed, but this time for quite a different reason. She stooped down and gave the lanarkite a kiss on the top of her head and invited her in for a little refreshment.

After assuming a more traditionally formal attitude and exchanging the Realmgreeting with the young humans, the elderly lanarkite accepted on one condition. Teodor would need to keep any treasonous opinions to himself.

* * *

Idocrase Station Four,
Idocrase System, the Realm

It was the second lunch break of the first shift at Kiezlyne Realmcare Clinic -Idocrase Station Four.

Thresher had just purchased her meal and sat down in the company cafeteria. She was soon joined by one of her fellow employees.

"Can I sit here, Citizen?"

"Please do."

"Nice to get away from the craziness for a while. It's Thresher, isn't it?"

"Yes, Thresher Korzeniowski and you're Amice. ... Amice Banwyns. Am I right?

"You're right, Thresher. You have a good memory."

"Comes from traveling so much."

"How are you enjoying your first day, Thresher?"

"This lunch isn't too bad, Amice."

"You'll find it's a little like working at Kiezlyne. It gets worse the longer you're here."

"Have you been here long?"

"All my life!"

"Well, thanks for putting up we me earlier. This is my first time at *Idocrase* and I just don't know all the local customs yet. I think I made a few social blunders."

"No harm done and don't worry, you'll soon get to know all our little peculiarities. The ettringites have a belief that when you're exceptionally bad, you get sent to a place of never ending humiliation and torment after you die. You must been very naughty to end up here."

"It can't be that bad."

"Oh, no? We'll convert you to a [full fledged] follower of the *Holy Arts* in no time. ... Never mind my bad attitude. I understand that you're mated to an Earth human. That must be amazing. I heard they still have vestigial tails. Is that true?"

"No. Teodor doesn't have a tail. He wears clothing, can read, and I think he has the concept of fire down pretty well now. And I think you're having a bit of a laugh."

"I am. Around here I'm known as the clown, but don't worry, I *usually* don't mean any harm by it."

Now, the two human females were joined by another. An older and less friendly looking one.

"Excuse me, Amice. I need to talk with our new med tech. So go somewhere else and eat. ... Now!"

"Is there a problem, Citizen?" Thresher asked the new arrival as pleasantly as she could.

"Yes, there most certainly is. I know you're new here, so I'll just give you a little warning this time. You need to understand the way things work around here. You're paid to handle the foreign races and the nobodies. Geertje, Amice and I handle the Company people and especially those connected with the Original Families. Understood? If we get behind, like after one of the Company picnics or meadowball competitions, then I'll let you know. Until then, you just do your little menial job and let your betters take care of the important patients. ... Oh, and it's good to meet you, Trisha. Welcome to Idocrase System. I'm your senior supervisor, Iseut Sceluwaerd. ... One more thing: word got around that your mate is some sort of writer or some nonsense like that. Just keep it clearly in your mind that those of us who run things around here also have the honor to be descended from this system's Originals. We don't like being looked into by some [two-bit] investigative reporter. So, find your mate something worthwhile to do and tell him to keep his eyes and ears closed or it might get very unpleasant for the both of you. Understand me, Trisha?"

"Yes, ma'am. I understand you very well. My name is Thresher and If you want to join me, please do. Otherwise, may I return to eating this delicious meal?"

"Be back at work in seventeen ... correction, sixteen minutes, Thresher."

It was later that day, that Thresher committed a grave sin. She had been instructed to help Amice expedite her treatment of a Company manager who had given himself a sore wrist by overdoing it at meadowball on his days off. Instead, she had rushed out to help an elderly cerargyrite female that had just fallen outside on the walkway and was bleeding profusely.

"Thresher, get in my office. Now!"

"You wanted to see me, ma'am?"

"You damn well know I do! You were told to help Amice, not some destitute old nuisance out in the public area. When I give orders, by the Gods, I expect them to be obeyed! We have even cheaper workers than you to take care of the charity cases. ..."

"They were all busy and she had abrasion injuries with acute hemorrhage ..."

"Don't interrupt me! Oh, and another thing. I thought I told you to keep that mate of yours out of our business. I just found out he's out in the public areas snooping around. If he doesn't mind his own business, you'll be out of a job and he is going to need medical attention more than that worthless old cerargyrite. Do you understand me.

"I don't believe what I just heard. That dear elderly female Citizen means nothing to you. What about your code of ethics. I don't need to stand here and listen to you. You ... you ... decedent of twice damned old sycophants!

Thresher stormed out of Sceluwaerd's office filled with the strength of righteous indignation. After getting only part way through the clinic she started shaking and crying. She pushed past Amice's attempts to calm her down and walked out of the clinic, forever.

Meanwhile, as Thresher was experiencing her first and last day at Kiezlyne Realmcare Clinic, her mate Teodor was out seeing the rather limited sights on *Idocrase Station Four.*

After a hour or so, he found a little [greasy spoon] and thought he'd get himself a [little nosh.]

When Teodor entered, he found that it was very crowded and the only place to sit was a table just big enough for two human sized Citizens—over on the very far end of the room.

Other than a few stares, his presence seemed to cause the locals no concern, so he walked over and took the seat with the more gregarious view.

Teodor felt the place was rather homey. Everyone present was human and when a living human waiter brought him his printed menu, rather than a robot with an interface, he started to feel he had finally found that little bit of Earth out here in the wilds of the Realm. The homeyness of the place would soon change, when, a short time later, he made an unusual acquaintance.

The door opened and Teodor glanced up from the menu to see someone come in and retrieve a take-out order. The funny thing was, that when the door was open, Teodor could have sworn he heard someone singing what sounded all the worlds like [European] Opera. The door closed and the singing stopped and so he reasoned that he had imagined the whole thing.

He hadn't. Now, the door opened again and an ettringite male entered. He was still singing, but a little more subdued. After he had a quick look around, he stopped singing entirely and walked over to what was now the only open seat in the place.

"Good day, Citizen. Would you be kind enough to switch seats with me?" then seeing Teodor's puzzled look the ettringite added, "I always feel safer with my back to the wall and my face to the door. Thank you so very much, Citizen. Our Imperial Majesty!"

Teodor thought the visitor was just about to sit on his lap and so he hurriedly got up and offered the seat to him. Apparently, it never occurred to the ettringite that the human might actually say no. Teodor took the remaining seat. The one that now left his unguarded backside open to the nefarious schemes of any that might enter the premises.

The ettringite had barely placed himself in his seat, when the waiter rushed over and saw to his needs.

"Good day, Most Excellent One. Please, order anything you wish. Our cook-staff anxiously await the privilege of serving you. Do you require a beverage at this time?"

"Thank you, Citizen Tygo, but I think I'll wait and have my beverage brought with my meal. I'll just need a few moments to decide. Thank you."

"As you wish, Most Excellent One! It is a pleasure to serve you. You need only to signal you're readiness and I will hastily return."

"I'm ready to order now." Teodor said to the rapidly retreating waiter.

But it was to no avail. The waiter didn't even turn around. He just shouted his reply, "I'll be back with you as soon as I can, Citizen!"

Teodor's old personality returned just long enough to assail the waiter with, "I'm so sick of this stinking Realm. You can't even order a meal unless you know someone. No class distinction among the united Citizenry—[My ass!]"

The ettringite looked a little embarrassed by his tablemate's outburst and seemed to take great pains to adjust his place settings and to find a comfortable way to sit in his seat.

After they had both settled down, the ettringite leaned over, and as he sniffed Teodor's neck, he said, "Thank you again, Citizen. That was very kind of you to relinquish your seat to me. I hope I didn't upset you."

"You're welcome. Must be nice."

"I'm sorry, Citizen?"

"You're obviously a somebody. Must be nice to be treated with so much respect." Teodor explained.

"I don't know what you mean. I'm just a fellow servant ..."

A young human male approached and [sheepishly] asked permission to interrupt the ettringite with a request. On receiving permission, he continued, "Most Excellent One, I'm so sorry to trouble you with trivial matters. ... I'm concerned with my piloting examination. It's coming up soon, and I had hoped to secure the blessings of the Most Holy Gods. ... I know that a sacrifice presented by one of the Exalted Race has far more influence than that of a mere human's. If you could trouble yourself to present this to the Priest. ... It is my prayer and a gift for the Holy Place."

"Citizen Parynghoot, I would be happy and honored to present this to the Priest on your behalf. From what I've heard, you will need little more than your own knowledge and skill to pass your examinations. But still, I will be happy to pass this along with your request and loving best wishes to the Priest. I hope I will see you at the Holy Place tomorrow night?"

"I will be there, Guard Lieutenant Commander Friso. And thank you for your kindness to one so unworthy, Most

Excellent One."

After the human humbly, but happily took his leave, Teodor, now quite humbled himself, addressed his tablemate, "Guard Lieutenant Commander Friso. I'm very, very sorry about that Citizenry remark. I'm just a little tired today. It was a very long and exhausting trip over from *Dorallchar Station* via Cerdic-Three."

"Sorry you said it, or sorry you said it in front of me? Never mind, Citizen. We all say things we wish we could take back. How else do you think I can weed out the traitors and the saboteurs?" the ettringite said with what Teodor took to be an amused look. He further explained, "Of course, that's really not my job at the moment."

"Thank you for not taking offense, Guard Lieutenant Commander Friso ..."

"Please call me Citizen Friso. I'm not in uniform."

"Thank you, Citizen Friso."

"You must be rather new here. May I please see your identification, Citizen. ... Thank you, Citizen Teodor Korzeniowski. Now, you know what I do, what do you do to support yourself, Citizen Teodor Korzeniowski? You said you just came over from *Dorallchar Station*. Do you work for RealmRock?"

"I'm a writer. My mate is a med tech and when she transfers from one station to another, I come along and look for new subjects for my books and stories."

"That sounds very exciting. I can guess you already know you'll find lots of things to write about here on *Idocrase*. Not that the locals will be too thrilled to find you in their guilt riddled midst. Eighteen hundred years is hardly enough time to soothe their troubled thoughts and certainly not time enough for them to welcome any close inspection into the colorful history of their esteemed ancestors. Not that an ettringite should have anything to say on the subject."

"It looks like we've come to the right place."

"Not to be personal, but I do have to say that your accent is a mystery to me, Citizen Teodor. Where are you from?"

"Earth."

"How did you ever find yourself in the Realm."

"I was one of those earthlings that the Clinohumites offered candy to ... I mean, enlisted a few years ago."

"I remember that. Now, I think I can just pick out a little Clinohumite-like accent. You do know that there are considerable bad feelings between the humans of *Idocrase* and the humans of Clinohum? I'm sorry to say this about my fellow Citizens, but I don't think you and your mate will find this place very supportive of your long-term health. I might even have to say, that in my official capacity, I would advise you to keep the knowledge of your involvement with Clinohum a complete secret and make rapid preparations to leave this system just as fast as you can. I mean that, Citizen Korzeniowski. But first, since you're from Earth, can you tell me what the words to this amazing song are all about? I understand they are in the Earth human language."

For the next few minutes both the human and the ettringite forgot about ordering food and instead Teodor was treated to a rather outstanding rendition of *Ich bin das Faktotum* from *Der Barbier von Sevilla*, by Gioachino Rossini.

* * *

Thresher was finally getting over the incident of the day before. When Teodor had returned home, she had filled him in on her adventures at the clinic and he had once again started to overreact, but this time, something held him back and he settled down and comforted her as much by his strength and self control as he did by his loving, kind and encouraging words.

One good thing, was that they had wisely secured a day-to-day hotel room instead of a leased apartment and so they were under far less financial pressure this time. They would still need to ask her dad to pay for their tickets if they were going to leave this system, but that could wait a few days and in the meantime, Thresher could see if any of the independent clinics were interested in taking a chance on a [loose cannon] like herself.

Teodor was still asleep and Thresher used her time alone to give careful thought to both their present situation and to their apparently unachievable long-term goals. She was determined not to let any setbacks change the attitudes her dad had so carefully instilled in her, or damage the relationship she had with her mate. No, they would see this through. ... Her thoughts were interrupted by someone at the door. "Well, the last time I was this desperate, it had been that kind elderly lanarkite. Maybe this time it will someone just as nice." she thought as she opened the door.

It wasn't an elderly female lanarkite. It was two uniformed male humans.

"Are you Citizen Thresher Korzeniowski?"

"Yes I am."

"I am Citizen Plathyez and this is Citizen Zoetelync. Our Imperial Majesty!"

"Our Imperial Majesty! Please come in. ... How can I assist you, Citizens?"

"We are station security agents. Here is my identification. We've come to inform you of a serious complaint that has been lodged against you."

At this point, Teodor came in, and identifying himself to their guests, sat on the couch next to his mate.

"Iseut Sceluwaerd, the day watch supervisor at the Kiezlyne Realmcare Clinic, has informed the station authorities that you made threatening statements to her and that you also accosted her in culturally derogatory terms. She also charges that your mate, Teodor Korzeniowski, is a [rabble-rouser] who has spent his time on station clandestinely trying to undermine the unification of the Citizenry and the authority of the Realm ..."

Thresher could see that Teodor was getting angry and was about to say something, so she quickly spoke up, "*Liebchen*, please let me handle this." Then she apologized to the security agent for interrupting him.

"You must understand, Citizen. That these are very serious charges that have made against you. It has also been brought to the attention of the station authorities that recently your mate, Teodor Korzeniowski, made statements about the Realm in a highly offensive manner. Specifically, "I'm so sick of this stinking Realm. You can't even order a meal unless you know someone. No class distinction among the united Citizenry—[My ass!]""

"Teodor!" Thresher gasped.

"I'm sorry, Thresher. And I'm sorry, Citizens. I was very tired and for a moment I just forgot myself. It won't happen again. I promise you."

"I'm glad you didn't try to deny it. You were overheard by no less than twenty witnesses. Citizens, the station authorities feel that since neither of you are currently employed, and that you do not appear, by your own words and actions, to be happy living in this system, perhaps it would be best for you to leave at the earliest possible time. Where you choose to go, will, of course, be up to you and of course, as Citizens of the Realm, you do have the right to remain here if you wish, but if you do so, it will be necessary to bring this matter to the attention of the Guard ... "

Teodor angrily interrupted the security agent, "Damn right we'll stay here if we want to! My mate didn't ..."

"Teodor, please! ... Thank you, Citizens, for bringing this matter personally to our attention. We agree that it would be best if we found another place to live and work. You may assure your superiors that we will be leaving in the next few days. Now, if you could excuse us, we have travel arrangements to make. Our Imperial Majesty!"

"Thank you for your coöperation, Citizens. Our Imperial Majesty!"

* * *

It had been a day since Thresher and Teodor had been visited by the station security agents, and still, they had been unable to come up with a way they could afford to purchase tickets out of the system.

Once again, someone was at the door and Thresher hesitatingly went to answer it.

"Amice. What are you doing here? You shouldn't have! You might get in trouble!"

"It's all right, Thresher. Sceluwaerd sent me. I'll make it brief so it won't look like I'm getting chummy. The station's political officer stopped by and talked to Sceluwaerd. He's being transferred and before he goes, he wanted to clear up a few things. Remember that cerargyrite you treated? She went to the station authorities and sang your praises loud and long. It seems to the [big shots] around here that what you did for her was the perfect example of what our Imperial Majesty calls a "Unified Citizenry." Since you were working for the clinic at the time, the Kiezlyne Realmcare Clinic is getting a Citizenship award. ..."

"Of all the injustices!" Teodor exclaimed.

"Teodor! Not now. Please, let Amice talk."

"The Political Officer seems to concur with your opinion, Teodor. That is why he insisted that Citizen Sceluwaerd help pay for this little going away present."

It was a voucher for two single economy trips from *Idocrase Station Four* to Boulanger-Four and an additional voucher for two sub-economy trips from Boulanger-Four to *Admiral I Taisto Station*.

Chapter Seventeen
Retirement Plans

Planet Palagon, Proculus System, the Realm

Guard Captain Evert got off the lift twelve floors early. This way he could just happen to walk by the Protector of the Realm's offices. The High Admiral was away. It had left several days before on the IGSS *Eviscerator* to take command of the investigations in the Wolnyn system.

"It's a shame Frida wouldn't get a chance to meet High Admiral Karen," Evert thought to himself as he approached its offices. "But there was little choice. Teodor was becoming a real danger to his mate Thresher and someone had to go and have a nice long talk with the human male."

To someone that didn't know Evert, it would look like the older ettringite male was just stopping by with the intention of flirting with the young and pretty ettringite female who usually sat at the desk outside the High Admiral's offices. Sonja was very pretty, but that was not what Evert had in mind. He had been on the receiving end of several of the High Admiral's parent Wilymia's chastisements, and so he knew a little of what the young Guard officer must be going through. Today, Sonja wasn't there, but Guard Lieutenant Commander Akio was and so although Evert missed out on giving comfort he did get a chance to talk over old times.

Evert was just finishing up the story about the time he and Akio had helped out Maurus with a difficult smuggling case when he heard, coming up from the lower decks, the sound of a voice that could only belong to his mate's cousin.

Evert had a good idea why Cousin Friso was in the building, and he also knew Friso always brought *fortesgrr* and snacks when he visited. So he hurried back to the lift and then up to his department's offices to wait for him.

Evert had just finished the customary interchange of greetings with his co-workers, started his interface, and spread out a few important looking documents across his desk, when he was alerted to Friso's unmistakable presence out in the corridor.

"Hey, it's 'The Sniffer.' Good to see you, Friso. What brings you over our way?"

"Good day, Trun. Just stopping by to see Evert."

Guard Lieutenant Commander Friso entered the office that Guard Captain Evert now shared with several other officers in the Imperial Majesty's Protection Detail.

Friso quickly looked around and seeing no one outranking his cousin-in-law, shared the Realmgreeting with him. Then, after exchanging the customary ettringite greeting, he sat down opposite Evert and offering to share the contents of his take-out meal container, got down to the business at hand.

"You know, I really hate that nickname!"

"They wouldn't call you 'The Sniffer' if you would just stop smelling non-ettringites."

"You would be surprised what you can learn about your fellow Citizens if you just stop and smell them. Take for example this human male that I recently ..."

"I would really rather not get to know how the other races smell, *especially* humans." Then leaning over, he whispered, "I'm told humans smell worse than a wet lanarkite."

"Hey, now!" came a voice from across the room."

"I'm sorry, Caoimhe."

Friso smiled and corrected his cousin-in-law, "I'm sure you know you're exaggerating, Evert."

Am I? You should sit here when Guard Commander Caoimhe returns from a little walk out in the rain."

"You know he's only having a laugh, ma'am. He's just jealous. Everyone that meets you thinks you have the cleanest, shiniest, and softest looking fur in the whole of the

Guard, if not in the whole of the Realm."

"Thank you, Friso. Now, you see the abuse we lanarkites have to put up with from you duo-chromatic giants."

Now, in an even quieter voice, Evert added, "First time I have heard us called giants. Caoimhe needs a telescope to see if our beloved Imperial Majesty is smiling or not."

"How are Klara and Frida?"

"Klara is very well, thank you. She's really enjoying it here on Palagon. You know, this is my first planetside posting since we've been mated. As for Frida, ... well, she seems to be doing all right in the Guard. At least with her fellow ettringites. Oh, Frida, what are your mother and I going to do with you? She failed another diversity review, Friso. This makes seven failings out of eleven tests."

"That is not good, Evert. Perhaps you should cut down on your own particular brand of humor. You know, we don't always realize how our jokes can effect, or even hurt others."

"Do you think I went to far with Caoimhe?"

"Maybe a little. Remember, Evert, she can't tell you off. You're her superior."

"She could file a complaint."

"Not if she likes you. And who doesn't like good-natured Evert. If only he would stop making those painful jokes."

Evert got up and walked over to Caoimhe's desk. "I'm very sorry, Caoimhe. I truly am and I will try very hard not to do it again."

"That's very kind of you, Guard Captain. Like Guard Lieutenant Commander Friso said, I like you. Everyone in the department likes you very much."

"Thank you." now returning to his cousin-in-law, "Friso, do you think it's all my fault with Frida?"

"Probably not, but you could have unknowingly exasperated the problem. Now, what is to be done about it?"

"Frida has an old friend from university—a human female named Thresher."

"The same Thresher you had me watch over for you, out on *Idocrase Station*?"

Yes. And thank you very much. I cashed in some goodwill and got Frida assigned to something quite out of her job description. She's going out to see Thresher and her mate Teodor. And then she's giving them a little warning. Teodor is quickly on the way to getting the adjective 'radical' added to his name in the files. That wouldn't be good for either of them. Frida's job is to help them see the danger, before it is too late."

"And Frida likes these humans? That's a good sign."

"Frida has known Thresher for a long time, and I think she really does have affection for her. We both know that owners can have a great deal of affection for their pets. It doesn't mean they think of them as equals. As for the male, well, I got the strong feeling that none of Thresher's old school friends think much of him. He is a little hard to like. He was among those humans that the Clinohumites brought from Earth to help them convince their own population to work harder at hating our Realm and every ettringite in it."

"From what I know of Earth technology, I doubt Teodor had ever heard of ettringites or the Realm before he met the Clinohumites. So, he only has their word against our good conduct. When I met Teodor on *Idocrase Station Four*, I found him rather personable. He even helped me translate this wonderful Earth human song that I heard recently."

"Still another reason to dislike him. ... I'm sorry, Friso. You're a good friend. Even if you do sing too loud or smell everyone in sight. I was surprised when you communicated over and told me they were heading over to *I Taisto*. What happened with that job the lanarkite found on *Idocrase*?"

"You forget the history of the humans of Idocrase."

"I don't know ... Oh, The One! I was just so happy to find out that Thresher got that job. I forgot about Teodor."

"Actually, it wasn't Teodor. Thresher is just too nice a Citizen to last even a few days on that accursed station."

"I never even considered that."

"They could extend their stop on Boulanger-Four and find a job there. If not, did you manage to find them something on *Admiral I Taisto Station*, or maybe on Anker?"

"Frida did. Then I just needed to give Thresher a good reference. She'll be *highly* recommended for job at a clinic during the pilgrimage. I wish you could have found them a direct to *I Taisto*. If Thresher finds work on Boulanger-Four that would be great, but I wouldn't know what to do with Frida. It's too late to change our plans now."

"I'm am sorry about the stop-over, but I paid for their travel arraignments the best I could. I would have liked to have been able to provide them with better arrangements and accommodations, but I just paid out a rather large deposit on my retirement plans. As it was, I had to convince someone else to go in with me on the vouchers. The important thing was I got them out of that system before I was transferred. Without my being there to protect them, I'm not sure how long they would have stayed out of trouble."

"I know you did your best. You always do, Friso. Thank you, again. You're a good friend. And I'll pay you back today. But what's this about retirement plans? You're still a little young to be worrying about things like that."

"I'm old enough and I'm tired. I know you'll laugh, but I got a really great deal on an old junked inter-system transport. It needs a lot of work, but the hull is solid and the engines work most of the time."

"How big a ..."

"An Epz9200—model two."

"That's a ship, not a boat!"

"I didn't say it was a boat. What good would a boat be to a inter-planetary transport company."

"I always thought you were missing a magnet or two in

your containment system, Friso. I suppose you'll pilot the thing yourself while giving recitals of Earth human songs."

"I already have a pilot in mind. He just needs to finish school first. Now, as much as I would like to stay and keep you from your work—I've still got work of my own to do."

"New assignment?"

"Yes, thank the Gods. I put three years of my life in at *Idocrase* and other than the time I pick up my ship, I hope to never see that odoriferous place again."

"Well, with this stolen mining torpedo to deal with, they're pulling in all our best investigators. Where's the new assignment? Out on the border with the Clinohumites? Or looking for the greedy and disloyal Citizens who tipped them off to its existence?"

"Do we have any idea who took it?"

"RealmRock made a mistake and shipped it over to Acm with a bunch of old equipment. Some pirates waylaid the freighter. When help finally arrived, everything was gone."

"That's not good. Can it be used as a weapon?"

"The High Admiral thinks it can. Now, the whole Realm is going to be turned up by its ankles and shaken. The Guard will be there if anything falls out of the pockets."

"Not me. I'm going up to *Palagon Station* to look for human internal organs. Nice job. A little macabre, but simple enough. Security thinks that two young cerargyrite males might have been stealing the contents of dead humans from the morgue. The station authorities are afraid of what will happen if they start to run out of already dead humans."

"I'm sure you'll sniff out the villains in no time, Friso."

"Goodbye, Evert. Please send my love and well wishes to my lovely cousin Klara. Don't worry about Frida, she's just like her dad. A little rough, but still not a bad sort. Goodbye, Caoimhe! Let me know if he doesn't behave himself."

"Goodbye, Friso. Take care of yourself." Caoimhe replied.

Friso was singing again as he walked to the lift.

Chapter Eighteen[71]
Admiral I Taisto Station

Hessite System, the Realm

It had been a long trip from Boulanger-Four, and the economy carrier Port Leyken Spaceways was not known for its comfortable accommodations. Teodor and Thresher were two very happy humans when the *AS20-14* was finally cleared for docking at *Admiral I Taisto Station*.

For the last one hundred twenty-three hours they had spent their time aboard, commuting between cramped seats, an over-used hygienic station, and a poorly managed prefabricated food purveyor. Had they splurged on entertainment screens, they could now have seen the beautiful planet Anker hanging like a blue jewel below the station. It would have been anticlimactic anyway, for now, all they could think of was finally sleeping on flat beds and washing up in water dispensing bathing units.

{"Warning! Warning! This vessel is in violation of the First Protocol! Warning! Warning! This vessel is in violation of the First Protocol!"} the announcement devise at the docking portico jarringly informed the chafing passengers and crew of Port Leyken Spaceways' transport *AS20-14*.

"Damn it! This nonsense again." exclaimed Teodor, recognizing the near demented and tinny sound of that universally deployed machine voice even before the meaning of its frantic words sunk in.

"Twice damn it! Stir it around, spread it out, and damn it again!" Added Thresher. As the daughter of a Fleet chief crewperson, she was always good for an impromptu metaphor.

"That's a new one, Thresher." Teodor said with a laugh as a robot herded them down the passageway to queue up at quarantine booths. [The pitch of that agitated machine's voice and this queuing procedure always made him feel he was at Hell's Department of Motor Vehicles. He wanted to yell out, "I just want to get my license renewed"][72] but he never did. No one, including his mate, would have understood the reference anyway, so why bother. Instead, he would end his plenitude of travel hardships as he always did, by meekly imitating a cow waiting patiently in line at a meat processing facility.

{"Next Citizen!"} a more controlled and therefore supposedly more soothing disembodied voice commanded.

"MOO!" Teodor rebelliously replied. He thought to himself, "Why was it that Port Leyken Spaceways never mentioned in their advertisements their complete inability to properly handle the paperwork for multi-system travel."

{"Next Citizen!"}

Thresher had once told Teodor that the First Protocol had come into effect almost eighteen hundred years ago. "Maybe now would be a good time to tell the *kripslods* at Spaceways." he thought to himself.

Quarantine scanning didn't hurt at all. Deliberate, or continued violation of the First Protocol could hurt quite a lot. If it was determined that the violator was indeed a threat to the [closed system] that was the Realm, then, the threat would be eliminated by the vaporization of the offending party.

Thresher tried not to give that any thought as she underwent the scanning procedure. It never worked. She always had a little tinge of an idea in the back of her mind that some overzealous quarantine device would detect a minute parasite in her body and save the whole of the Realm by eliminating the offending prokaryote and the organic vessel it traveled in. Needless to say, she hated quarantine scans and was very relieved to exit safely on the secure side of the unit.

"Identification, Citizen?" The Guard junior crewperson demanded.

Perhaps, it was knowing that she was once again on the safe side of the scanner, or perhaps, it was knowing that officially her long trip was finally over—whatever the subconscience reason—Thresher was very happy to hear the polite, but formalistic, interrogational voice of the Federal Police Agent. Her happiness showed, and the human male Guard junior crewperson was quite taken back. No one was ever happy to show their identification. He was bored, she was pretty, and he would have flirted with her, had he not seen the ettringite Guard first lieutenant, in the summer walking out uniform, watching him from the reception area.

"What was your departure point, Citizen?"

"Boulanger-Four"

"Any stops on route?"

"None, that I was conscience of. It was booked as a nonstop to *Admiral I Taisto Station*, Anker. Is anything wrong? My mate and I had tickets for an express. If we wasted time in that [tub] picking up ..."

"Thank you, Citizen. You may enter the station. Next!"

Thresher passed into the reception area and stood looking around for Teodor. There was no sign of him. "Probably still hung up in queue." she thought.

"Thresher Korzeniowski, may I have a word with you?"

It was an ettringite female in some form of white uniform. Being brought up in the Fleet, Thresher was accustomed to quickly looking over the rank and branch insignia of those she met.

"Certainly, Guard First Lieutenant, what can I do ... Frida? Frida, it is you? It's so great to see you again! Wait, are you on duty? I mean is this official?"

"It's so good to see you again, friend Thresher. Let's find that mate of yours and go have some drinks together. Have time?"

"We'll make time. How did you know we were coming to *Taisto*? Wait, I can guess. You talked to my dad didn't you. No. Your dad talked to my dad and this is official business isn't it. Official family business. ... There's Teodor." Thresher waved her mate over.

Teodor had, as usually was the case, gotten into the wrong line. This time he was just behind the old Citizen with the hearing problem, who was also far too vain to ever think of getting any form of treatment for what others thought was his 'condition.' Behind Teodor was a young ettringite professional that was so lost in thinking about the business deal he could be making, "If only these stupid tourists would get out of my way," that he got into the scanner with Teodor. The mess took a good deal of time to straighten out and reminded Teodor why he truly disliked dogs and especially yuppie dogs.[73]

Teodor spotted Thresher. He also spotted her companion and thought, "Oh joy, another dog!" Then he spotted her uniform insignia, "Oh joy of joys, a Guard dog!"

He managed to confine his ever growing appreciation for his life and the universe in general to his mind and used [auto pilot] to speak with his wife. "*Liebchen!* Looks like you beat me through quarantine again. Any idea where our luggage might be?"

It was Frida who answered, "I think the distribution area for your transport is number six. Over there on the left of the vending area."

She could read the human's unhappy look at seeing her, mixed with perhaps more than a little bewilderment, and so she thought to herself, "Thresher, what did you get yourself into. I wonder if this male can even write his own name."

Using another of his obscure Earth references, Teodor spoke to the white uniformed Guard officer, "Thank you, Citizen. What brings you to *I Taisto Station*? Did you come here for the waters, also?" [74]

"Teodor, what are you talking about? This is my old university friend, Frida." Thresher corrected.

"Oh, the one who burned the hole in the professor's lunch?" Teodor asked, looking at the ettringite.

Frida answered, "No, that was Fuzzi Eck'crawd, and it was a physics lab floor not a professor's lunch. I'm the one who turned off the dorm lighting control systems while trying to override the security sensing units."

"We'll, I'm sure you have honed your breaking and entering skills by now. It's said, criminals make the best police. ... I don't want to be rude, Frida, but Thresher is overly tired from our trip. We'll be on station for several days. Maybe we can catch up with you some other time."

"Teodor! Don't be a *kripslod!*" Thresher shouted.

"See what I mean." Teodor informed Frida.

"Teodor, I am going to get our stuff and head over to our lodgings. Then after I have cleaned up, I will meet Frida for food and drink—mostly drink. If you want to join us, you may." Thresher walked off to retrieve their luggage.

Frida was enjoying the show. "Maybe when you clean up you can see if your host has one of those tools some of you human males use to make your faces all smooth and shiny. I hate to tell you, but your fur is coming in all blotchy and uneven." Frida said, [sophomorically.][75]

"I'm sorry, Frida. I didn't shave recently. It's a little hard to accomplish that task when you're crowded into a malfunctioning hygienic station with your feet soaking in some other being's urine." Teodor responded.

"You have to love Port Leyken Spaceways. They add poor quality to undependable service and serve it up at barely more than their competitor's prices. Next time you should get a better transport for Thresher. Then you could send yourself RSDS. They have great deals for livestock." Frida said with mock helpfulness.

"You know, if you were a male they would call you a

dog." Teodor said under his breath in English as he headed over to assist Thresher with the luggage.

Guard First Lieutenant Frida hurried up along side of Teodor and whispered, "I have big floppy ears and at the academy I got high marks in Earth cultural and language studies." Then she added in passable English, "When later we go out, if you behaving, maybe I will purchase for you a banana, ... boy monkey!"[76]

"A touch!" Teodor thought. Had he finally met his match? "Never!" But he would have to be careful with this one.

* * *

Teodor Korzeniowski decided to join his mate and her friend at dinner. After a thorough body scrub and a change of clothes, the problems of the past seemed to melt away. He was now ready for whatever the Realm could throw at him. He felt he could even handle a charming evening sitting in a restaurant with a bipedal Doberman pincher who dressed like she should be selling frozen confections, or tickets to the secret police summer dance.

It was hardly just a restaurant. *The Princess Agrippina Room* at the RealmStandard Hotel, was considered one of the most elegant dining establishments in all of the Realm. The decor was from the time of that Princess of beloved memory, with a just a splash of the romantic bygone days of the Imperial Space Fleet.

One of the qualities what set it so far apart from all its many contemporaries was an uncanny ability to serve the varied tastes of all its multi-species patrons without causing any to have discomfort or objections. Thresher had a selection of the finest Anker seafood and Frida found the aroma of her friend's meal so faint as to hardly interfere with the pleasant smell of her own selection of raw organs of *rafn*.[77] The slightest hint of a sauce camouflaged the extreme freshness of the ettringite specialty from either of the humans. Teodor was by custom rather a strict 'root and fruiter,'[78] but even his plate was so superbly arranged, that it would have tempted a cerargyrite.

Ettringite etiquette discourages conversations during the actual eating process, and so Thresher had to wait several minutes to find out what prompted her old dormmate to treat them to a meal in so upscale an establishment. Teodor finished his extensive meal last. He might be forgiven for over-partaking of Frida's generosity. After all, he had hardly eaten anything on the five day trip from Boulanger to Anker.

Since he had begun traveling with Thresher, Teodor had added greatly to his knowledge of the culture of food in the Realm. For instance, he now knew that a Port Leyken Spaceways' transport ship was an even harder place to find a meal customized for a strict herbivore than even a space station inhabited primarily by cerargyrites. He also learned, most importantly of all, that on every homeworld across the Realm there lives some form of single celled organism that consumes carbohydrates and excretes ethanol.

With that last lesson in mind, and in addition to the wine they had all consumed with their meals, Teodor finished his meal with what he thought was very nearly *aquavit,* while Thresher chose a syrupy dessert drink. Teodor thought Frida's *ag-brocht* looked like used lubricating oil and smelled like industrial paint stripper, but since she was paying, he thought he might like to order one next round.

No guest is ever rushed at the Realm Standard Hotel and so, with the main course cleared away, there was now plenty of time for snacking, drinking, and conversation.

Thresher started, "Well, Frida, thank you very much for treating us to this very fine meal. I hope we can return the favor soon. This hotel is incredible. Unfortunately, we had to find something a little more budget conscience." Then in a whisper, "Is this where you're staying?"

"This is the life, Thresher! For the next eleven days I have a suite up on the Iridium Level. The Ambassador from Phlogopite is staying just down the hall. I feel like royalty!"

"Being a Guard medical officer must pay pretty well." Teodor observed, then added, "If you females will excuse me, I think I'll go powder my nose."

Frida waited until Teodor was far enough away then asked, "Powder his nose?"

"I have no idea what that means" Thresher replied.

"Thresher, how are you and Teodor getting along?" Frida asked as she played with her drink.

"We manage. It's a little hard at the moment ... with Teodor not working. And my jobs have all been so temporary. It seems like all we do is travel from station to station and hub to hub, with a stop at a planet or two to break the monotony. It's interesting seeing the sights, but it can get tiring after a while." Thresher answered and then spent some time arranging her remaining table settings.

Frida didn't think it was right to keep staring right into her friend's face ,so she began to look around the room. "I like that painting. I could see it over the fireplace in that [manor house] that I'll own with my mate someday."

"Complete with great hall and a [ballroom.] Of course he'll look like [Ettring's] Crown Prince Hroderich." Thresher said, remembering the many times she and Frida had discussed their fantasy lives.

Frida just looked dreamfully at the picture for a minute; then getting serious, asked, "And how's your relationship?"

"We're doing fine, Frida. Teodor's cynicism can get tiring sometimes, but he's kind and he means well. I do love him, and I think I can truly say he loves me also."

"Of course Teodor loves you. Why else would he be willing to hang out with me tonight. I don't think it's my charm or my beauty that attracts him."

"It could be your generosity." Thresher said with forced

humor. Frida was on about something and taking far too long to get to the point. "Your dad's still an investigator isn't he. I hope he didn't send you here to prove me wrong."

"My dad's more concerned that his only daughter is a racist. I failed another diversity review. Thresher, do you think I treat humans as inferior?"

"Yes, of course you do. You always have. I've always just assumed it was the way you were brought up."

"You never said anything."

"It is a little awkward. I am a human. I think you know that. You're also a friend and I think you know that also. Now, what's the problem? I thought all you ettringites were a tad xenophobic." Thresher gave her friend a big toothy smile and hoped Frida would lighten up. Her mood seemed so out of place in so splendid a setting.

"My paternal grandfather was a member of *The Way of The One*.[79] He had religious gatherings in his house numerous times each month. Every species was truly welcome! For two years, he let a destitute human family live rent free because they were his 'brothers and sisters.' My dad never took to that religion, but he always lived up to granddad's views on the equality of all the races.

"Years back, my dad was assigned to investigate religious and racial intolerance in the Fleet. It cost him a few promotions, he even got death threats. Here I am, the offspring of tolerance, and I can't even bring myself to call a human—"

Teodor returned and sat down. "You both look sad. What's the problem, did you miss the life of the party?"

"Frida feels she might have acquired a reputation for disliking humans." Thresher answered.

"Bite somebody?" Teodor asked.

"Teodor!" his mate exclaimed.

"It's all right, Thresher. I guess I have to learn to respect your mate's pathetic attempts at humor. Teodor, you're from

Earth—tell me truthfully, do I really look like a dog?"

"Either God or Darwin has a worse sense of humor than I do. You are the spitting image of *'Canis familiaris dobermanis.'* Of course in the country I was brought up in, Dobermans have cropped ears, but in some other countries they have long droopy ears just like yours. But who cares what you look like to me." Teodor ended with an uncharacteristically warm smile.

"And I think you may have had a little too much to drink, Frida." Thresher sensibly added looking at her friend. "I've never known you to be overly concerned about what your family thinks about you. And what's the big deal about your races physical similarities to some Earth animal. I think you're down on yourself and the alcohol isn't helping."

The drinks were starting to catch up to Teodor as well and he was continuing a story no one else was still listening to, "You know it's funny to think about how some of the races look like Earth animals. I mean the halotrichites do look a lot like dinosaurs. I mean the way they used to be depicted, before they started talking about them having feathers and such. I guess the cerargyrites look a little cat-like—at least something in the face reminds me of a cheetah. Now what do palagonites look like? Again, maybe some kind of dinosaur. Like a long armed tyrannosaurus with fur.

"It's the thenardites that have me stumped. Something familiar about them. But I just can't remember where I saw something with a [tawny] coat and stripes just on the butt end. They are ugly! They look like they should be waiting in the forest for a little girl with a food container to skip by."

It was the comment about thenardites that brought Frida's thoughts back to the subject she had been sent to discuss with Thresher in the first place. Now, she realized it was time to get down to work.

"Thresher, when my dad suggested that I get over here to *Taisto Station,* and that I be the one to tell you about how very near to 'containment failure' your mate has gotten; well, I thought it would be easy. But now that I see how close you two are ... it is a little awkward.

"My old friend, Thresher, let's be very clear about one thing, I'm very happy to say that the security entities of the Realm have never come across any time when your mate was not loyal to you. His loyalty to his adoptive country is open to suspicion, but never to your monogamous relationship.

"To start with, my dad hopes you and your dad don't think he was trying to get either of you hurt with that job at RealmRock. You were never supposed to take the position. It would have been very temporary even if you did. What you weren't told at your interview was that the mine was soon scheduled for deäctivation. What my dad arranged with the understanding of his superiors was a way for you to start reäcquiring a better security status. It almost worked. It would have worked if Teodor had kept up the good behavior he started after your close communion outside the RealmRock offices.

"Now that I have met him, I think he did try. What messed him up was a human female that our human agents tell me was exceptionally good looking." Turning to Teodor she asked, "Remember that pretty red haired human female you met on RSDS Hub Cerdic-Three? While Thresher was in that interview with Crindon Agri?"

Teodor was sobering up rather quickly now that the dreaded Citizen's Court had convened. He wished it was even quicker, but he did manage to reply. "Yes I remember meeting a human there. She might have had hair that color. She said she was destitute and looking for help!"

Thresher stared at him. "That's strange, Teodor, I don't remember meeting her. I don't even remember you tell—"

Frida took back control of the meeting. "I think he believed her at first. She must have told you one great story of injustice piled on more injustice."

"She said her family had been swindled out of their home and that the local authorities were being far less than helpful. She, ... I think she told me her name was Jeltje or Jeltsje, something like that. Anyway, she told me that she had traveled out to Cerdic-Three to see an attorney that was handling a class action suit against the company that had defrauded her family. The lawyer was no help. He wanted money up front and she didn't have enough left—"

"I'm going to guess the lawyer was an ettringite and that she had a very good idea that, money or no, he had no thought of helping humans. So that's when you took her to a *very* public eating establishment, (Frida gave Thresher a reassuring look) and purchased her a meal. How long did it take you to realize she was a phony?"

"I knew that a minute into her story. I just figured she was starting out in the [confidence] business and was still learning the trade. It was like the time back on Earth, when I was waiting at a light and a woman with a baby in her arms walked up to me and asked for money to buy milk for the crying child. Only thing was, I saw her hit the baby and start it crying just before she approached me, so I knew it was some sick [confidence] job. I was all alone and in a part of town that made me very uncomfortable so I got away from her in a big hurry."

"This time, it wasn't a female abusing a child so you bought her lunch?" Frida was irritated. His Earth experience smelled of cowardliness and she hated cowards, especially when hatchlings were involved.

"I guess I didn't do the right thing either time. I'm not the big tough rebel I like to think I am. ... I'm sorry, Thresher, it was the stupidest thing I could have done. I violated your trust and I'm sorry. Very sorry! I wasn't looking to do anything with her! I just ... I was ... I wanted to look like a [big shot.][80] It was stupid, Thresher. *Liebchen?* Please forgive me. It will never happen again!"

Thresher didn't say anything, so Frida continued, "I wish that was the most stupid thing you did that day, but you exceeded it rather quickly—"

That last comment made Thresher look up and again focus in on her school friend's findings.

"—She wasn't an apprentice [confidence] artist was she? No, she was an agent from some radical human independence movement looking for fellow humans with anti-Realm leanings," Frida continued.

Teodor answered, "She was a Clinohumite agent to be exact. Messed up when she targeted me. I don't think she was expecting to find someone who had actually lived among her people."

"Teodor! Of all the brainless things you have ever done. A Clinohumite agent! She could have killed you on the spot. What were you thinking? What would have become of all our plans?"

Teodor unwisely interrupted with another of his obscure Earth references, "We're going to buy a farm on [a tropical island back on Earth]—"

"Teodor! I work so damn hard to keep us alive! ... I don't mind you showing a little kindness to those who really are in need, but if you ever pull a stunt like this again I will never forgive you!"

Frida added the topping, "He didn't report her. She was already under surveillance and was going to be arrested anyway. ... You didn't report her!"

"As I said, she seamed a little amateurish. It was just talk, she didn't do anything. I didn't want to get her in trouble."

"You just didn't want to see some human female get dragged off to some unspeakable [pit] and have her body broken by hulking monstrosities that get their jollies hurting others. We don't do that! Not in the Realm!"

Teodor shot Frida a look of cynical amusement, so she

continued, "I'm not saying that some over zealous security agent has never slapped around some uncommunicative suspect—no one claims perfection. Things happen and careers end. Torture is forbidden by the Protocols. The Protocols that all government operatives, police, Fleet, and Guard members swear to obey."

"I'm sure the Protocols also forbid Citizens being hunted for sport. Ask that poor *schlep* on Almand how that worked out for him! He was sentenced by one of your precious Protocol respecting magistrates to be first prize in a one-sided game of 'hunt the human!'" Teodor sneered.

"Teodor, where did you hear about that?" Thresher asked.

Frida answered for him, "I'll bet he read about it in the *Illumination of Solidarity!* He was glancing through a copy just a moment before that Clinohumite approached him."

"No wonder she targeted you! That's radical propaganda trash. I'm sorry, Frida. It's my fault. I should have taken better notice of what he was filling his mind with." Thresher responded—rather shaken.

"Thresher, I'm not your hatchling! If you'll still have me then I'm your mate. I may be a little unfamiliar with all the cultural subtleties here, but I'm not stupid." Then looking at Frida he added, "It did happen, didn't it? A human agri worker living on Almand did take some illegal medications and then in a drug fueled rage he did beat up a little halotrichite hatchling. He *was* found guilty and he *was* sentenced by a *real* judge in a *real* court of law to have the hatchling's family take him out to some quiet place and hunt him down like a animal. It did take several days of running around in terror before the human was finally allowed to die. Tell me when I'm wrong about your wonderful Realm and its tub full of idealistic Protocols." Teodor had nearly sobered up now and he was [mad.]"

"I don't know, but I'm sure that's not the whole story." Frida admitted.

After a few moments of awkward silence, Teodor finally replied, "Well, at least your honest. Probably, isn't the whole story. After all, the truth doesn't sell papers. I'm sorry Frida. I didn't mean to get mad at you personally."

"I'm sorry I got us all so heated up. This is a first class hotel, so please let's keep our decorum up and our voices down. Teodor, I think you need to learn quite a bit more about your adoptive country and you're not going to learn it from the *Illumination of Solidarity!* Just reason briefly if it would be reasonable for a civilization as multiracial and multicultural as ours to allow society to break down to the point where ... where public hunts and such things could ever be allowed.

"Teodor, I may not be the most diversity minded Citizen in the worlds, but even I would not sit idly by and watch my fellow Citizens of *any* race be held to the level of contempt that you seem to observe around you daily. Now please, you're stuck here with us, so stop feeding your personal delusions. Help your loving and patient mate find good employment. Raise a family if you two want, but by the love of anything you hold dear, just behave. And keep your opinions to yourself."

"Maybe someone needs to speak up." Teodor challenged.

"Speak up? Whatever you may think of the Realm, and whatever you may feel about the rights of sentient beings the universe over—do you really think it was striking a blow for the revolution by responding to a Junior [female] Realm Citizen Youth Guides' request for charity donations by suggesting that the hatchling ask our Imperial Majesty for one instead, "Because she looks like she could benefit from skipping a few meals.""

"Teodor, you didn't call our beloved Imperial Majesty fat in front of a [little child] did you?" Thresher asked in horror.

"I know I'm hardly Che Guevara, but I was just—wait a minute. Frida, who has access to my surveillance records?"

"Relax, Teodor. You don't think they would waste the time of our beloved Imperial Majesty with the ramblings of a dissatisfied, unemployed, and unlicensed layabout."

"Unlicensed! Where are *your* tags, Pup?" Teodor mockingly said in English as he defiantly stared at Frida."

"Teodor! ... Frida, please. I know you're trying to help, but please! Teodor does try. He's not a layabout. I do thank you, but I hope this little exercise of our emotions is over." Thresher requested, then after a moment, with a mischievous smile she added, "And anyway, he's not unlicensed. Being a refugee from the Clinohumites he still gets one-nineteen and thirty-seven a month from the Ofimdocs[81] whether he works or not."

Frida relaxed to find her old dormmate's lighthearted personality coming back. Even Teodor started to find his agitation subsiding just a little bit. After a few moments of silence at the table, Frida finally asked Thresher, "If I can give your emotions one more workout? You *now* have a job! It's temporary, but the pay's good and they'll put you both up for the duration.

"Remember Taru? Maybe not, she was a year or two ahead of us. Well, she and her parents own a clinic here on *Taisto*. They'll be needing extra staff as soon as the pilgrimage starts." Frida handed Thresher a data card. "Stop by the day after tomorrow. They'll be expecting you."

"Thank you very much, Frida, that was very kind of you." Teodor said trying to sound exceptionally sincere. Then he added in English, "Good girl! You get a cookie!"

"You don't need to thank me, Bonobo,[82] I just got here myself. No, I can't claim the credit for this good result. Your mate has worked very hard and unfortunately from time to time she has had to deal with a little impediment ... I mean disappointment in her life. This opportunity is only what she deserves.

"Well, hatchlings, that's all I have time for tonight. Now,

I'm going updeck and enjoy my officially provided suite. Can you find your way back to your meager lodgings?"

"Thank you, Frida. I think we can manage. Don't get too comfortable up there. I think this will be the last time you will need to intervene in Teodor's destructive behavior.

"Right, *Liebchen*?"

* * *

Teodor stood outside the Mirjami Medical Clinic on *Admiral I Taisto Station*. Thresher was inside talking shop with the proprietors and he was finding the subject a little intense this close to lunch. As it had turned out, Thresher did not remember Taru from university, but Taru said she thought she remembered her. She reasoned that with her fellow [alumina's] fine references and credentials she would make a excellent temporary addition to the clinic's staff. The fact that an additional reference had recently arrived and from no less a source than the Office of the Imperial Majesty itself, had cinched the deal. Thresher had no idea why the Office of the Imperial Majesty should have taken an interest in her finding a job, but then again, she had never actually sent her *résumé* to Taru in the first place. It would seem that Frida's dad had gone to a lot of trouble to help his daughter's former dormmate. Whatever the background story, at least for thirty-two days she would have a good job.

With all that had been put 'on the table' and additionally, with all that had been put in their glasses during that first dinner with Frida, Thresher and Teodor wisely slept late the next morning. Now that they had time to talk it over, Teodor promised to make an even greater effort to be loyal to his mate and supportive of her search for gainful employment. Thresher had agreed to hold him to those promises, and she decided to forgive him for his past misdeeds as well.

Later, Thresher had spent several hours brushing up on human and cerargyrite first aid procedures and Teodor watched parts of a Fleet History Day marathon of old war entertainment videos on the screen. He had never known just how many military conflicts the Realm had been involved in during its eighteen hundred year history and how much cerargyrite bravery and military genius always seemed to play a significant part in providing the Fleet with victory.

Much later, Frida met them for dinner and again she insisted on paying, "Just until you strengthen your finances." she had explained.

Tonight's dinner, once again at the prestigious *Princess Agrippina Room*, was far more conducive to proper digestion. Frida thought it might be fun to spread a little irritant into Teodor's wounds, but concluded that it would be in poor taste. With similar reasoning Teodor had resisted the idea of finding a stick and seeing if he could interest the Guard medical officer in a game of catch. Thresher liked *both* her dining companions and so did not need to swear off *any* affronts to good manners for the evening.

Still, the meal was not without interesting developments. About the third course, Frida noticed they were now in the presence of a highly honored fellow guest. "Thresher! Look over at the *maître d'hôtel* station. See who just came in!"

Teodor commented, "I hope it's a rabbit! This place could use some excitement."

Thresher didn't hear Teodor, she was too busy looking over the party that was being shown to a table past where they were sitting. "Is that Roopertti?"

"It is" answered Frida as she stood and intercepted the youngest of the three cerargyrites walking past, "Our Imperial Majesty!"

"Our Imperial Majesty!"

"Fleet Captain Roopertti. It's good to see you again, sir."

"Thank you, Guard First Lieutenant ...?"

"Frida. sir! My class in combat tactics at Guard Officers

Training School was fortunate to have you give us several guest lectures. This is my friend from university, the former Thresher Selverlinck, now, Med Tech Thresher Korzeniowski and her Earth-born mate Teodor Korzeniowski."

"I am pleased, Guard First Lieutenant Frida, that you remember me so many years after my amateur attempt at teaching. It is a pleasure to meet you two humans as well. May I present my honored adoptive Father, retired Fleet Chief Crewperson Heikki and my twice honored adoptive mother, retired Fleet Junior Chief Crewperson Seija. Citizen Teodor Kor ... zen ... iowski, Med Tech Thresher Selverlinck Korzeniowski and Medical Officer Guard First Lieutenant Frida.

The two senior cerargyrite's expressed their pleasure at meeting their fellow Citizens and then left their adopted son to tactfully end the conversation.

"Well, Guard First Lieutenant Frida, we will not keep you from your meal any longer. It is good meeting former students, especially ones that have matured into fine young servants of our beloved Imperial Majesty. Good evening." the Fleet captain said. Then taking his leave of the unexpected interruption, he continuing to escort his parents to their table.

When they had again taken their seats, Thresher leaned close to her friend. "Wow, I can't believe you did that. I'm not complaining mind you. What a handsome and well spoken officer—"

Teodor interrupted, "I didn't know you liked tall males with auburn fur."

"Jealous?" Thresher asked.

"Teodor smiled, "I don't know if I have ever seen a cerargyrite with that color fur before."

Frida gushed with awe, "I just know that we are in the presence of a living legend. Top in his class at Fleet Operations School. Awarded the *Fleet Medal of Bravery* while still a cadet. He saved his classmates and their training ship from murderous Clinohumite pirates with grand deception and an anti-matter torpedo right down their throats. Now, he's just been put in command of the TFSS *Predator*. He's the youngest commanding officer of a System Control Vessel in the history of our Realm."

Talking about her hero, Frida failed to notice the older cerargyrite female that approached the table. The humans did see her and Teodor gestured for Frida to turn around.

"I hope we did not seem rude." retired Fleet Junior Chief Crewperson Seija apologized. "My adopted son has so many well wishers, that it gets a little difficult for us to spend any time alone with him. It was very kind of you, Medical Officer Guard First Lieutenant Frida, to take so respectful notice of him and I wanted you to know that your attention was not unappreciated by his adoptive father and I."

Teodor stood and offered her a seat. He had a little knowledge of cerargyrite customs, so he tried, "Gracious Mother," and not possessing a tail to twitch, he added a slight bow of the head.

The cerargyrite seemed to understand the meaning and the gesture. "What a gentle being. Thank you. I can only stay for a short time. I did want to ask your mate a question. Thresher, many years ago when I was studying engineering I had a dear human friend. She was newly mated and her name was then, Sanne Selverlinck. Her mate was a Fleet Crewperson, Carsteloot Selverlinck. It was so many years ago and I am sorry to say that we lost contact. I was wondering if you may be related in some way."

"She was my mother. My dad is still alive, but my mother was killed on duty when I was still a little child. That was over thirty years ago. It's nice to know you still remember her so fondly after so many years. You must have been good friends." Thresher responded with tears in her voice.

"I am so sorry, young one. Here I am bringing sad

memories into your lovely evening with family and friends. ... If you are going to be around Anker for a few days, perhaps, you all could come down and visit with my mate and I. If it would not bring you pain, I have some memories of Sanne that I would like to share with you. Here is our address. Do you think that you, your mate, and your friend could come?"

"It's painful to miss my mom. But it's also good to remember her and the life she shared with my dad and me. Of course we can come. Can't we Teodor?" Thresher rarely ever talked with Teodor before making plans, but in the presence of this distinguished representative of the home planet of the cerargyrites in the Realm, it seemed like the conservative thing to do.

"It would be an honor." Teodor assured her.

Frida acknowledged her agreement with a passable imitation of a cerargyrite gesture of willing agreement.

Then, as it looked like the cerargyrite might leave, Teodor asked, "I'm not originally from the Realm, so if this question is out of line please let me know. I noticed your adopted son has an unusual color of fur."

"I'm not offended by your question. It's a long story and I really need to get back to my family, so I'll make the story short. You can hear the rest when you visit with me on Anker. You see, I am unable to have children of my own, but my mate has always been very supportive. Although I always knew that he was disappointed he would never have a son to see grow up to honor his family with deeds of bravery and sacrifice. One day, I was praying to The One, that He[83] would grant me the strength to endure my limitations.

"I could hardly have imagined that at that very moment, a little orphan child hid among the lifeless remains of his family. The Clinohumites had come to the aid of the Gehlenites and together they were driving the occupational forces of the Republic of the Cerargyrites out of their system. A family friend [Tymorann Alphrontex] just happened to be passing by and came upon the wreckage of a military transport. The only survivor was a little child with the coloration peculiar to the families that ruled the Republic. It took the child and brought him to me on Anker. The One had wondrously blessed me and given me far more than I had prayed for. It has been an honor and a pleasure to raise The One's gift as our own son. Now, unless I want my son to come looking for me, I had best take my leave from you Citizens and get back to my own family." With that she got up and returned to her own table on the far side of the room.

"Wow indeed!" Teodor exclaimed. "What dignity and what old fashioned faith. I've lived here five years and that's more religion than I've heard in all that time. I mean even when we got legally mated the judge didn't mention gods more than once or twice. Now I've heard about prayers, gods and miracles all in one conversation and a hurried one at that!"

"*The Worship of The One* is the official religion of the Realm, but even so, it tends to be treated like quaternary duty"[84] Frida explained using a obscure term she then had to explain to the Earth-born human.

"So what else do I need to know to fit in around here during the pilgrimage" Teodor asked with a laugh.

"Our little guy is all grown up. Who gets the duty of explaining religion to him, Thresher?" Frida joked.

"Don't ask me. I only took a few years of Re-Ed class because it was required to get into university. Frida, didn't you tell me that your paternal grandfather was a *Way'r*."[85]

"I also said my dad never took much interest in that religion. No, I'm at a loss here. I never learned much about my people's old Gods and even less about the thenardite's new one. That's it! Speaking of my paternal grandfather, maybe Teodor can hang around in the station's main concourse until someone hands him a copy of the *Journal of the Way of The One*. That would be a good start, I mean if he really wants to know about gods and such. And by the way Thresher, I do know they don't like the term '*Way'r.*' Dad told me they find it offensive."

"Sorry!" Thresher said meekly to no one in particular.

"I remember you just recently making me promise not to accept any literature from strangers." Teodor protested.

"Oh, this stuff is safe. Not officially sanctioned, but tolerated." Thresher explained.

"All right and the pilgrimage is that a Realm thing or just something the adherents of that religion celebrate?"

"Which religion?" Thresher asked. "Oh you mean the *Way of The One*. No, it has nothing to do with them. In fact, they never celebrate anything that promotes the creäted, only the Creätor. As for the Government of the Realm — there is absolutely no official support for the pilgrimage. There couldn't be. Our Imperial Majesty supports racial unity and understanding, not intolerance and prejudice. No, except for providing additional security, the government has nothing to do with what will happen here.

"I think the custom of traveling to Anker, and later to this station, just sort of happened. After the civil war was over and the Realm was established and finally brought peace again, well, the remaining humans just started bringing their children to have them see the statue of the Citizen most responsible for their lives. After a few centuries, the superstition started of presenting the new humans to their protector: the High Admiral of the United Forces, I Taisto. Now, it may be, more or less, just custom only. My parents brought me here when I was a month or two old. I don't think it was to let a long dead war hero see me, or to condemn the memory of equally long dead ettringites. It was just something human families do." Thresher tried to find a way of explaining it to her mate, but thought she probably failed. She didn't know that on Earth most of the holidays had evolved into little more than a reason to purchase candy and [greeting cards.]

Teodor knew exactly what she was talking about, but he still had some questions, "Let's get back to the ettringite involvement in all of this in a moment. For now, let me get this straight: Right now, I can go to a public walkway and openly receive a copy of a publication not approved by the government, and promoting a belief system that is at least partly in disagreement with the official religion of the Realm. I can also return to this station in a few days and take part in a celebration that violates principles of thought and conduct as promoted by the Imperial Majesty and the government of the Realm. Lastly, I can do all of this without bringing upon myself the displeasure of the State. Very good, when do we all start shouting and breaking furniture? I mean, is this all some way for our rulers to let us take a break from mindless obedience and let our hair hang down?" Teodor said, returning to his old habit of sarcastic cynicism laced with obscure Earth references.

Frida looked long and hard at Teodor. She almost thought of finding out if any of his apparent mental or emotional deficiencies had a noticeable odor. In the end the distasteful thought of sniffing a human overcame her curiosity and she limited herself to verbal dialog. "You have lived in the Realm for five years and you don't know [diddly] about our history, our customs, or our religions. I thought only a Citizen by birth could be that ignorant. As I said before, I'm not much on religion, but I think I can at least give you enough background to save you embarrassment.

"Let's start many, many, thousands of years ago, when the palagonites were the biggest bullies in the known universe. When they came upon a new race, they enslaved them, or ate them, or usually both, and they did this with dozens of races. In time, they found the thenardites and attacked them.

"The story goes that the thenardites appealed to their god and The One gave them total victory over the palagonites. The would-be conquerors were forced to beg for mercy. In the end, the thenardites introduced their religion to their former attackers and the palagonites enforced those beliefs over all their vast territories. I think it was only my people that did not take to this new religion [en masse.] We stubbornly clung to *our* old assembly of Gods, Goddesses and assorted supernatural creatures. As time went on, the thenardite religion was molded to fit the various treasured beliefs of the Empire's many residents and became *The Worship of The One*. Today, it conforms to what the members of *The Way of The One* say was the original thenardite religion in name only. So that new religion promotes a return to what they say are the beliefs and values of the ancient religion.

"Now for my race's sordid tale: Thousands of years ago we sent some explorers to Earth and brought home some of the indigenous fauna. Much to our eternal regrets, included among that fauna were specimens of humans. With the passing of time, you grew in number and went from curiosities, to pets, to slaves, to clever (but decidedly dangerous) enemies of our ettringite way of life. My race decided to exterminate your race—including all the Earth humans as well. Most of the races that made up *The Empire of the Palagonites and the Peoples of the Galaxy* didn't coöperate with what we ettringites thought was a reasonable and well thought out system of genocide. A civil war broke out, the Empire was destroyed, and High Admiral I Taisto kicked our collective tailless butts. Some thenardites were invited to put together a new system of government and *The Thenardite Brokered Federation of Planetary Republics and Political Bodies* was born. Becoming a benefit to every being in the universe with the exception of Teodor Korzeniowski.

"The cerargyrites built a huge statue of their favorite son

and the humans started worshiping it. Today, the ettringites produce as much value for the Realm as any other member race. Still my noble race gets treated like we are collectively guilty of numerous unmentionable crimes. Despite what you will undoubtedly hear many times during the pilgrimage — my people are not as a whole just waiting for a second chance to eradicate your people. Some of us, the delusional ones I'm sure, know humans they consider as friends and others that they tolerate." Frida stopped talking and leaned forward to kiss Teodor on the side of his face.

They both resisted the urge to shudder.

* * *

A few days later, they all traveled down to Anker and visited with their new friends. Several days after that, Thresher was hard at work at the Mirjami Medical Clinic and Guard First Lieutenant Frida was on route to Avalite to meet up with her ship the IGSS *Eviscerator*.

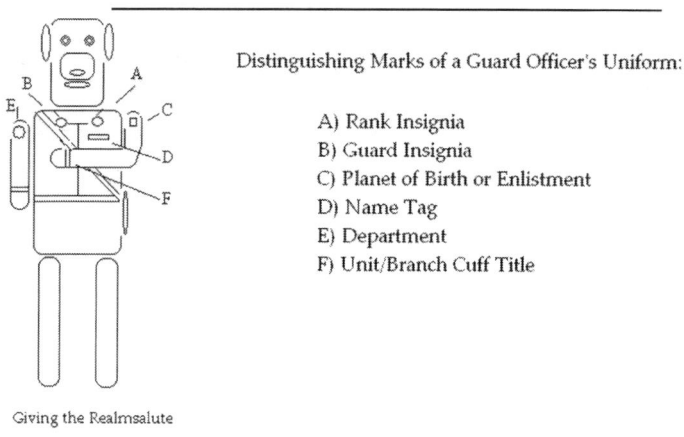

Giving the Realmsalute

Fig. 3 This is a rather poor quality recreätion of an example of a CET illustration from a Fleet cadet training manual. CET stands for: caricature, ettringite, typical. CETs (both official and nonofficial) are common in the Realm.

Chapter Nineteen
The *Cult of Adalheidis*

Planet Ettring, Adalheid System, the Realm

Contented and sleepy after his meal, Gunter sat back against a tree. His host was also very relaxed and he seemed to be fast asleep against his own tree. Some of the *hrunjer*[86] had ventured out from their hiding places and were cautiously moving closer to their favorite grazing area. After Gunter had killed one of their flock, the other *hrunjer* had scattered to the far areas of the enclosure and hidden beneath or behind any cover that they could find. Now that the carnivores had finished eating and were apparently satisfied, they were once more returning to their usual daily activities of eating, defecating and sleeping. "What simple creatures these *hrunjer* are." Gunter thought. "They have no idea that they are trapped inside a structure. They think this is the whole world, not just a sophisticated 'stage setting' built in the backyard of Fleet Admiral Sigsteinn's mate's ancestral home. It is an amazing re-creation. Hard to believe it is only a few hundred meters away from the noise and the crowds of a main thoroughfare in Ettring's largest city."

The Fleet admiral stirred himself and some of the herbivores were startled and ran off. Sigsteinn looked over and addressed one that remained very close by and was greedily eating a particularly delectable plant. "Stick around and get nice and fat. I'll eat you soon enough, my [epicurean] friend.

"Excellency, this is an amazing place!"

"Amazingly private, Member Gunter. We can talk freely in here. Now, since we are both well fed, perhaps it would be best if we discuss the matter at hand. Please, my friend."

"Member Aldric has successfully fulfilled his mission in

the Wolnyn system. He has acquired an Xz-7 for us and has placed the blame for its disappearance on human agents acting in the interest of the Clinohumites. Just to be on the safe side he made certain [Realm Citizen] Alwer Geeraerd died in a very incriminating way. Alwer is that human vermin who has been passing secrets to the Clinohumites for years. Secrets that *we* have been most carefully feeding him."

"Very good, Member Gunter. I understand from official communications, that all [the Realm's] military forces are out looking for the Clinohumite pirates who are believed to have the weapon in their possession. Member Aldric has done very well and you did very well in selecting him.

Thank you, Excellency. It is a great honor to strive together with you in the service of our Great Goddess. I have still more news that I hope will be equally pleasing to you, Excellency. That fool Haimo has finally done something right and has secured an old mining tug that Member Karsten can use to get close to *Guard One*. It is a shame Member Kuniberaht has to die along with that blasphemous Imperial Majesty. He won't live to see all our ... all your plans come to fruition."

"When Guard Captain Kuniberaht was diagnosed with his terminal illness, the only concern he had was how he would be able to end his life in the service of the Great Goddess. I can think of no better way to begin one's journey to eternal bliss then by assisting in the destruction of that mocker of the Gods, that twice damned Imperial Majesty of the Realm. ... Without his sacrifice, I don't know how we could have ever achieved our goals. But, you are right, Member Gunter, he will be greatly missed."

"I'll have the transponder codes for the Port Leyken transport soon. Adal is back with us and has made certain the Clinohumite pirates will be interested in the *AS23-11*, when the time comes. Should we be concerned that there may be many of our fellow ettringites on board when the human scum commandeer the ship?"

"Not particularly. Our Great Goddess will protect them if she feels the need. ... But what was that about Adal?"

"Member Adal has been in hospital. Nothing serious, but I took the precaution of having a member on Acm keep an eye on the situation. If Adal had become a liability, he would have been taken care of very quickly."

"Was he ever unconscious or out of our sight?"

"Never, Excellency. I made precautions. His interface was secured and his codes were changed—just to be sure."

"Good work! As we both understand, accidents do happen. Therefore, at this critical time, I'll need to add myself in your portable interface. Just in case I need to take over your duties during the final phase of the operation."

"Certainly, Excellency. Should we set the codes in front of them?" Gunter asked, pointing to the grazing herbivores.

"Very amusing, Member Gunter."

Gunter retrieved his portable interface from among the clothing that he had removed prior to hunting down their meal. He now navigated through the many redundant high security settings using his biometrics and his audio codes. The portable interface was now ready to accept the identifications of additional users that might need access.

Fleet Admiral Sigsteinn let the device sample his scent and other biometric markers, then he concluded with a simple but effective protection against any sophisticated genetic based subterfuge. Not that any was currently in use by the security services of the Realm, but one could never be too careful and anyway there were always those rumors about what the accursed unholy thenardites were capable of.

"Sigsteinn. One, Seven, Five, Star, Tee, Zed, Three, &, Two, Nine, Nine, One, Double-U, Four, ~, Six, Six, Four, Six,"[87]

With these precautions completed, Sigsteinn and his guest put their clothing back on, and after locking up the private hunting area, returned to the house. An hour later, one of the

Fleet admiral's servants helped Member Gunter get his shuttle back to Tephro.

* * *

Later that night, Fleet Admiral Sigsteinn found he was having trouble sleeping. He kept thinking about thenardites and especially about their rumored ability to take on the body of the creatures they ate. It sounded like tales told to [children.] But what if they could? Sigsteinn got up and quickly dressed. He retrieved his sidearm from the lock-up in his [study] and woke Anzo—the servant in charge of his private hunt. Together they went out and checked the security systems. Only Anzo had used the door to the hunt since it was last secured by Sigsteinn several hours before.

They entered the area and Sigsteinn methodically lighted every single *hrunjer*. Then, they checked the carcasses against the inventory and it matched perfectly. The Fleet admiral gave the area one more inspection and finding everything to his liking, went back to bed. In the morning, Anzo would dispose of the carcasses and restock the hunt.

Fleet Admiral Sigsteinn could now get some sleep. Gunter had brought wonderful news. Soon the Imperial Majesty would be dead and the humans would get all the blame. As Sigsteinn lay in bed, he had pleasant thoughts of humans running about in terror in his now greatly enlarged live hunt area. He fell asleep with a smile.

A short time later, the *real* Anzo woke up on the floor of the Fleet admiral's private liquor storage area. His brain hurt and his mouth tasted like two week old floor sweepings, marinated in vomit. All he could remember of the last twenty-five hours, was a dream about a talking *hrunjer* getting him even drunker and drunker. Better not to let his employer know anything about his misappropriation of the costly *ag-brocht*. He dragged himself to his feet and quietly and very secretly returned to his quarters.

Chapter Twenty
The Privateers of Clinohum

A Clinohum Republic military installation

"Captain Dieuwe, what would you say was the Realm's most effective weapon?"

"If you're talking about the one that causes us the most difficulty, Admiral Renstaes, I would have to say it was their Interloper drones. Five times in the last few months they have put one of our ships out of action. Fortunately, each time we had other ships in the area to provide defensive assistance. If we didn't work in packs we would be helpless against them."

"But, operating in packs limits our scope of activity. We only have so many ships, and it's too restricting using them all grouped together. Now, what do we need to solve this problem?"

"Admiral, if my engineers could get their hands on an Interloper's control system, we should be able to develop effective countermeasures."

"Unfortunately, Captain Dieuwe, they have always managed to self-destruct before we could secure one. ... What would you say if I told you that one of our agents in the Realm has managed to get hold of a damaged, but still interfaceable, control and communication unit from a current production model of Interloper drone?"

"I'd say our prayers have been answered. That is *if* we can successfully get it back here without anyone in the Realm knowing about our having it."

"Interesting, Captain Dieuwe. Why do we need to keep the Realm ignorant of our acquisition?"

"There is nothing magical about an Interloper, Admiral. If we can find a way to interfere with their sensors or internal workings then we can render them less effective, or perhaps even ineffective. However, if the Fleet finds out we have one to tinker with, they will just speed-up their research and development that much faster. It will be expensive for our enemies, but in a short period of time we will be right back where we are now."

"The control unit in question has been kept stored away at a manufacturing plant on Acm for three months. They're awaiting instructions for secure disposal. In the very same storage area is the reconditioned positioning pod of a Gl-895 transport. The pod is soon being shipped out to *Palagon Station* on Port Leyken Spaceways' *AS23-11*."

"And the Interloper control unit will be hidden inside?"

"Exactly, Captain Dieuwe. After it leaves, our agent will falsify the documents to show that the control unit was inadvertently shipped out to that great waste dump at Idocrase. By the time the Fleet gives up looking for it and reports it missing, we will have already tipped our hand by our ever more audacious interference with the Realm's civilian shipping. As you said, eventually, they will up-grade their Interlopers. But then, we will just be back to where we are today. No worse and perhaps far better off."

"We will need to be certain that the waylaid transport is not rescued until well after we have had time to carefully retrieve the control unit."

"Just prior to you waylaying the *AS23-11*, my squadron will attack a freighter convoy between Avalite and Dignite. If the situation allows, maybe we'll even hit *Dignite Station* as well. That should keep the Fleet very busy. While they're concerning themselves with us, you put the crew and passengers off somewhere and take the transport to a quiet and lonely place to remove the control unit."

"I think I'll keep the crew and passengers with me. A hostage taking operation will give me better cover."

"As you wish, Captain. We get underway at 14:00 hours."

Chapter Twenty-One
IGSS *Eviscerator*

Planet Palagon, Proculus System, the Realm

Guard Captain Evert returned home from his last day working in the Imperial Majesty's Protection Detail. He brushed the snow off his [great coat] and sat down on a bench just inside the common entrance door for his apartment building. Even after so many years as an officer in the Guard, he still kept himself in excellent physical condition, so it was emotional and not physical overexertion that necessitated the pause before joining his mate in their apartment. He had done it again. And this time, his mate hadn't even been able to unpack completely from his last disciplinary reässignment.

"She is a wonder!" he thought, thinking about his loyal and long-suffering mate. They had first met back when Evert was still a very junior clerk in an unexceptional law office on *Boulanger Station,* and Klara was a low paid and over worked science teacher at a university preparatory school on the planet Acm. At the time, Evert was attending a supplementary after-work-hours school that facilitated one becoming an officer in the Guard without the usual need to attend a six-year course of studies at the Guard Officers Training School. Klara's cousin Friso attended the same school as Evert and he introduced them to each other at a holiday party.

Three years later, they were a legally mated pair and Evert had finally been accepted into the Guard office of the Political Police. A year later, their daughter Frida was born. Evert dutifully did his assignments and up through the ranks he climbed. All the while, Klara steadfastly submitted to a life of living on stations and of long separations from her mate.

Something had happened to Evert when he finally achieved the coveted position of Guard captain. He became disillusioned—but Klara never changed. Even after Frida attended university and Evert's attitude started to effect the quality of the assignments he was entrusted with, Klara never complained. She just quietly did more packing and unpacking.

Now he had done it again—and just three months into the first planetside posting he ever had. What a posting! A senior member in Department Six (the Imperial Majesty's Protection Detail.) Complete with a nice apartment in a building half way up Mount Chert, overlooking Pearl Sands Bay, on Palagon. Pearl Sands Bay! They still weren't in the position to have their own detached dwelling, but this was an entrance to a social strata neither had ever dreamed of experiencing.

Now, Evert had foolishly tried to help his daughter's university friend, Thresher. He had gone much too far and his career was truly over. He had thought that being made to leave his mate, for what was supposed to be a year's deployment on a mining asteroid, was the worse his superiors could do to him, but now he had his doubts.

Maybe it was time to finally retire. They could move to a subsidized living center out on some RSDS hub. There, they could spend their retirement complaining about the state of their health to their fellow old and bitter neighbors. They might also find time to complain that Frida never settled down and produced grand-children for them. All the while, they could live out some other Citizen's glamorous life with the help of the entertainment screens.

Evert's thoughts now turned to his daughter, "Frida! What will we ever do with darling Frida?"

Frida had been born when Evert was just a Guard first ensign assigned as the second assistant to the political officer on a Fleet support station out at Allemontite—near the Gehlenite border. Housing limitations prevented Klara from joining her mate right away and so their daughter was born on Alunite while Klara was temporarily living back home with her parents. Klara and Frida wouldn't be able to join Evert for almost two years.

When Frida was four years old, the family needed to split up once again, with Guard Second Lieutenant Evert going to a posting on a PCV and Klara and Frida again living with Klara's parents. Evert liked his in-laws and was comfortable with their non-religious secular viewpoint. So when Frida was six and ready to start primary school, Klara joined Evert while Frida stayed with her maternal grandparents to attend an exclusively ettringite school on Alunite. "Maybe that wasn't such a good idea." he thought, chastising himself.

For most of the next twelve years, Frida lived, learned, and grew up, within the ettringite population on Alunite, only occasionally traveling out to stay with her parents near one of Evert's postings. What could Evert expect with Frida growing up surrounded by only ettringite members of the Realm's multiracial Citizenry. By the time she attended university, Frida had begun to show signs of the corrosive influences of classic ettringite xenophobia. He had hoped the more heterogeneous atmosphere of university life on Phenak would correct the effects of the first eighteen years of her life, but it didn't seem to. Then she started sharing rooms with a human named Thresher and Frida's anti-human prejudices slowly began to show signs of softening.

After graduation, Frida applied to and was excepted at the Guard Officers Training School. While she was at school, Evert and Klara, with the support of her councilors, had encouraged her to take additional courses in human studies. It had been interesting to see how she handled that two year course in Earth human culture. She did very well, despite the fact that she always remained the only ettringite and practically the only non-human enrolled. A few years later, when her former university dormmate Thresher had met an Earth-born human named Teodor and decided to mate with him, Frida had advised her against it. Still, in a move Frida's parents found most encouraging, she redoubled her efforts to learn the convoluted aspects of Earth human culture and history.

After the humans became a mated pair, Frida had spent considerable time learning the difficult Earth human language, 'English.' She had felt that this would allow her to better understand and converse with Teodor. Her high marks and praises from her instructors had even allowed Evert to secure permission from his superiors to use his her to warn the Earth-born human about his dangerous radical tendencies. Evert had thought that being back together with her old human friend might have helped his daughter deal with her apparently deep seated anti-human feelings, but just a month later, she did it again.

"Oh, Frida! Why do you keep messing up on your diversity reviews. What was it she did the last time? Oh, yes, she called a human, 'Furless Flat-Face!'[88] It was a [set up] and it was arranged to test her. But still! No amount of provocation should have incited such an acute racial slur on your part. Oh, Frida! What are your mother and I going to do with you? Where did we go wrong?" Evert said, repeating out loud his most recent communication with his daughter to the empty common area.

Guard Captain Evert's conversation with his absent daughter was interrupted by the unexpected appearance of his old friend, Guard Commander Reto.

"Hello, Reto. This is a surprise. Our Imperial Majesty!" Evert said while he traded customary ettringite greetings with his co-worker.

"Our Imperial Majesty! Good day, Evert. How are your containment fields holding up. Steady?" Reto asked in a very sad and concerned tone of voice.

Both the ettringites were momentarily distracted from their conversation by an unusually intense flash of lightning. As it was fading away they both turned at the sound of someone else entering.

"Evert, I'm so sorry!" exclaimed Reto's mate Elsa, as she came (from the snow storm raging outside) into to the warm and dry common area.

"Thank you both for your concern, but this isn't the first time I've been reässigned. It will be hardest on Klara, but we'll manage."

For just a moment Reto stared at his friend. Then he finally asked, "What? You don't know do you? Of course we're sorry to see you moving, Evert. But that's not why we're here to see you and your mate.

"Elsa, maybe you should go up and visit with Klara while Evert and I have a little time alone together. We'll be with you two in a little while."

"What's going on, Reto?" Evert asked, after Elsa left them to go up and see Klara.

"I'm so truly sorry, Evert! I hate to be the one to tell you. ... The *Eviscerator* got into some trouble near Digenite. Pirates again—and this time they did some damage."

"Frida?"

"Nobody knows. The pirates hit a freighter convoy a third the way between Digenite and Avalite. They must of hoped to bring the Fleet out from *Digenite Station* so the station would be an easier target for a raid. They couldn't have known a system control vessel and its battle group was that close behind the convoy.

"Two of the freighters got lighted up very badly and all the pirates scattered when they picked up on the *Eviscerator* approaching. At least that was what everyone on the SCV thought. Guard Senior Captain Aelius sent over a medical team and a repair crew to the worst damaged of the freighters. A pirate ship was hiding in the debris just behind it. There was a fight and the pirate ship got it far worse than it gave it. The pirate ship couldn't take any more light so it engaged its gravity drive. The boarding shuttle was pulled into the graviton ..."

"Frida was on the shuttle?"

"She was in command of the medical team. ... Evert, there is no evidence the shuttle crashed into the pirate ship. The debris field has been thoroughly scanned and there is no sign of the shuttle. If it hit the ship there should be evidence of at least the ship's destruction if not the shuttle's. Fleet Intelligence has this theory that could explain how the pirate's small attack ships can manage to get back aboard their mother ships so quickly when we go out after them. They think they may have a way to bring them aboard though the middle of the graviton stream. Our shuttle could be on the pirate ship right now."

"Thank you, Reto. You are very kind, but why would a combat damaged ship bother to take the time to bring aboard an enemy's shuttle? No, my beloved Frida is gone."

"Listen, Evert! I'm not just giving you a false scent. Frida was on a boarding shuttle. A [heavily armored] boarding shuttle! Even the most massive ship the pirates have ever used against us—not even the *Vengeance*—could hope to continue on under its own power after sucking in an [Esker] class boarding shuttle. I say again, there is no debris from the shuttle and very little from the pirate ship out there. Additionally, what debris has been found has beam damage all over it. Beam damage, not impact damage. I know it's not confirmed, but we still have to believe there is at least a good possibility that the shuttle is still intact."

"How can I tell Klara her little child is gone forever!" Evert exclaimed, collapsing back onto the bench.

Chapter Twenty-Two
The Waiting is Over

Political Police Headquarters, *Aegerite Station*
Proculus System, the Realm

Guard Commander Sascha hated humans with every cell of her body. Still, it would not do to let her superiors in the Guard suspect that view, even for an instant. No, if she was to remain valuable to those to whom she was truly loyal, then she would need to appear the ever dutiful, diversity spouting, mindless automaton, that the blasphemous Realm believed her to be.

As she led the yellow-furred human female down the corridor to the office of Guard Admiral Reinier, she thought to herself, "The human said it had important information to sell concerning a possible Clinohumite attack on the Realm. And the Guard admiral believed the creature! Nonsense! Humans never have anything of importance to speak into the ears of their betters. Greed and lust seemed to be the only two topics they know anything about, and only a fool would willingly listen to their twisted jabbering on either subject. A white hot metal rod would make them speak cheaply enough. To pay for the crap issuing from their foul mouths was insanity. But Reinier was a *kripslod*, and if he wanted to *pay* to be subjected to lies and half-truths spoken by a vile creature that should be sucking vacuum and not wasting valuable ettringite air, well, so be it. The Taciturnians would know how to deal with brain dead old fools like Reinier and race traitors like Evert. Praise to the Gods! Praise to Adalheidis the Great One of the ettringites!"

"In here! ... Citizen." she said almost in a snarl.

"Thank you so much, Guard Commander Sascha. You have been very helpful and all too kind." returned the human as the door opened for her. Then, to the Guard admiral she inquired, "Guard Admiral Reinier, it so good of you to see me. Is it permissible for us to speak alone?"

"Guard Commander Sascha, has our guest been searched?"

"Yes, Guard Admiral Reinier."

"Then you may leave us. Our Imperial Majesty!"

"As you wish, Guard Admiral Reinier." she said and then saluted, "Our Imperial Majesty!"

Guard Commander Sascha walked back down the corridor to the office she shared with several other officers in the Political Police.

As she passed by his desk, Guard Second Lieutenant Hrolf looked around the room and seeing that they were momentarily alone, called her over, "What's going on with the Big Boss?"

"The timing couldn't be better, Hrolf. With that sacrilegious pilgrimage finally over, every human [nut case] has climbed down out of the trees and is jumping up and down, jabbering for attention. Aina from Field Work passed this particularly miserable specimen off on me and that fool Reinier almost fell out of his chair in his excitement at the prospect of having his time wasted by its idiotic chattering. It must be our Great Goddess at work. The timing is perfect. Reinier out of the way on this of all days." Sascha explained.

She started to walk away and then thought about her younger and less experienced co-conspirator, "Hrolf, keep your mind on what your doing and don't get sloppy. Everything depends on us all seeming to be doing our jobs and doing them right."

"Yes, ma'am. Only four hours to go."

Just then, Guard Commander Orvokki rushed into the office and excitedly tossed her travel pack onto her desk. Seeing her and wondering if they had been overheard, Sascha said, "Quiet, Hrolf. Keep your eyes off the clock." to

Orvokki she added, "Hatchlings, always planning for their after hours recreational activities."

"Did you two hear the news?" Orvokki asked. "The Federals just arrested some attendant at an ettringite Holy Place on Tephro. They cracked his interface and found a detailed plan to use some sort of mining torpedo to assassinate our Imperial Majesty. It's supposed to happen today—when she travels over to visit the *Excarnator*. The Military Guard just arrived downdeck—"

Orvokki was interrupted by instructions from the building's communication system, {"Attention! Attention! All Guard personnel assigned to the Political Police and visitors to these premises. This is an internal security inspection. All weapons are to be placed in a safe configuration and left at the owner's duty station. All Guard personnel and visitors are to wait in the corridors for an internal security inspection. This building is now under security containment. Give full coöperation, regardless of rank, to the Military Guard personnel now inspecting the building. By order of the Protector of the Realm, High Admiral Karen. Our Imperial Majesty!"}

As the announcement was still sinking into Hrolf's mind, Sascha was drawing out her sidearm and not with *any* intention of placing it in a safe configuration.

The shock grenades concealed in Orvokki's travel pack exploded and sent all the room's occupants down onto the deck unconscious.

And now over at:

Fleet Traffic Control, Proculus System, the Realm

"Fleet Traffic Control, Proculus System, to Port Leyken Spaceways' Transport *As23-11*."

{"*As23-11* receiving you, Traffic Control. Requesting docking, Port Leyken Spaceway's terminus twenty-four, *Palagon Station*."}

"Aelianus, keep them up and out of the way. Looks like we finally have some action from *Guard One*."

"*As23-11*, hold in outer system circuit spZ-n20. We will course your [navigational computer] shortly. We have priority traffic in system."

{"Traffic Control, this is *As23-11*. Please repeat instr ..."}

"*As23-11*, repeating, hold circuit spZ-n20. ... Damn it! Past the mark. Reconfiguring pattern. *As23-11*, you're in past your mark! Slow to 761 and hold to outer system circuit spZ-r3. Repeat hold to spZ-r3. Acknowledge, *As23-11*. *As23-11?*"

{"T ... afic Cont ..."}

"*As23-11, As23-11*. Switch to communication setting C-94. Repeat, communication setting C-94!

"*Guard One*, we have unresponsive commercial traffic inbound to station. Please change to path spR-ww14. You are cleared for docking, Fleet Dock—bay five. Your [navigational computer] has been coursed accordingly. We'll let the machines sort this out."

{"*Guard One* to Fleet Traffic Control. Acknowledged."}

"*As23-11*, please acknowledge. You are off course. *As23-11? As23-11? As23-11*, we are coursing your [navigational computer.] Are you receiving data? Are you receiving vocal?"

{" Traf ...Contr ... distorted ... down ... inoperable."}

"Sir! No confirmation from *As23-11's* [navigational computer.] They are still a long way out. Hit the panic button? Or, just give them some time to [re-boot] their systems? Your call, Fleet Second Lieutenant."

"Let's give them a few minutes, Aelianus. If they pass am6 let me know. ... On second thought. If they pass am6, push it and then let me know."

"*As23-11*, this is Fleet Ensign Aelianus, Fleet Traffic Control-Proculus System. Let's try this again from the beginning ..."

"Communications, this is Fleet Second Lieutenant Drusus

at Traffic Control. Please see if you can get me anyone over in Data Systems ... and also put me through to Port Leyken Operations. One of their transports is having issues—again!"

"*Guard One,* you need to pick up the pace. You're still outside of ww14. *Guard One!* We have unresponsive inbound commercial traffic and you need to be on ww14."

{"Fleet Traffic Control, this is *Guard One.* Guard Captain Kuniberaht speaking. We are on a highest authorization inspection of the system. Please arrange it so we are not bothered by commercial traffic. Thank you. *Guard One* out."}

"Damn it, Aelianus, that's the Imperial Majesty' shuttle! What are you—"

At this point Drusus' chastisement of his junior was drowned out by an alarm. The *As23-11* had passed mid-system circuit spR-am6 and Fleet Ensign Aelianus followed orders and activated the System Emergency Alarm.

A short time later a small self propelled and course correcting object left the *As23-11* and headed towards *Palagon Station,* the Fleet repair dock, and *Guard One.* Fleet Second Lieutenant Drusus upgraded the SEA to a full System Defense Alert and all military ships and facilities in the system went to combat stations.

Fleet Repair Dock, Proculus System, the Realm

At Fleet Repair Dock, things on the weaponless and engineless TFSS *Excarnator* had also taken a troubling turn.

"Fleet Captain! System Defense reports the EnBeams are still inoperative." announced the jobless weapons officer.

"Ma'am, let me launch. With the EnBeams down, we're the only ones that can protect *Guard One!* There are no other warships in the immediate area!"

"Under no condition are you to take any squadrons out there. They'll have the EnBeams operational shortly and so even if you could safely launch, you'd just be in the way!"

"With all due respect, Fleet Captain Lady Lutgard—"

"Request denied, Fleet Wing Commander. Denied! ... Listen, Miki, in all of Fleet history no one has ever launched fighters from a ship *in* repair dock. I appreciate your loyalty and your willingness to defend our Imperial Majesty, but I can't let you do it. We'll just have to pray and wait for System Defense to bring the EnBeams [back on line.]

The ship's senior medical officer [Fleet Commander HRH Crown Prince Hroderich] entered and approached his recently announced *fiancée*, Fleet Captain Lady Lutgard. As he stood next to her chair, he readied to add his voice in one last effort to persuade the CO to allow the fighters to launch. But first, he questioned the BDO,[89] "Fleet First Lieutenant Florus, where is Fleet Commander Kenta?"

"The Executive is stuck on the dock with the Second, sir."

Fleet Captain Lady Lutgard added, "As a security measure I had the boarding tubes retracted. Is there something I can help you with?" Then in a whisper she added, "My love."

[Doctor] Hroderich put his hand on her shoulder and leaned in close to her ear, "Lutii, are you certain we couldn't use the docking correctors to clear our tail out far enough for a safe launch? If System Defense can't—"

"By our Great Goddess Adalheidis, not you too,[Beloved!] Please leave me alone. You must understand, I know wha—"

[Doctor] Hroderich now spoke with noticeable agitation, "Florus, please have the political officer come to the bridge with a security detail, immediately."

"Is there a problem, [Doctor]?"

"Yes! I've just committed a mutiny." [Doctor] Hroderich replied, stepping back to let him see the now motionless form of Fleet Captain Lady Lutgard. Then he spoke to the startled Fleet wing commander, "Miki, I have no authority in this matter, but if I were you, I would get down to the stern launch area. I think there's a good chance that Guard Commander Caelinus will give you permission to try and save our Imperial Majesty. May The One bless your efforts!"

Chapter Twenty-Three
Meanwhile, on *Palagon Station*

Palagon Station, Proculus System, the Realm

"Repeated laser blasts turned the ship's bulkheads into colanders dripping with molten metal. The security agent tried to get a line of sight on his heavily armed opponent, but it was too late! "Sweet Mother of Mercury, could this be the end of Stanislav Endicott!""

Teodor was sitting on a bench thinking about the detective story he was writing. Thresher crouched down next to her apparently napping mate and spoke into her cupped hands, "Earth to Teodor. Come in, Teodor!"

"Oh hello, Thresher! Hey! That was an earthling expression you just used. Good to see I'm having a positive effect on you. How'd the interview go?"

"Haven't gotten in yet. They told me it shouldn't be much more of a wait. I've got to get back up there, but I just wanted to let you know it could be an hour or so till I'm out. I don't have time to eat, but if you want to run off and get something over there, I'll wait around here if you're not back before I finish up. No sense both of us starving."

"Actually, I wouldn't mind tending to nature first. They must have a hygienic station in a big food court like that. You're sure you don't mind if I run out on you?"

"Not a problem, Teodor. I'll be fine. See you back here in front of the Cerdic-Chaidam Academy in ... let's say, two hours, all right?"

"All right ... and thanks, *Liebchen.* You're a brick."

"A brick?" Thresher thought as she walked back into the lobby of the school.

Teodor had spotted quite a few inviting food vendors on his way to the hygienic station and, now that he was relieved and refreshed, it was time to be refueled. "I've got money for a change. What to start with?" he said under his breath. 'The Interplanetary Palace of Dirty Silverware,' 'The Realmwide Conglomerate that Grease Built,' or the ever popular 'Fried Thing-atarium?' " He always missed joking around with his mate when she was off at work or more likely in an interview. So he found himself thinking of the little childish nicknames they had for some of the more universal eating establishments found on the many stations and hubs of *The Thenardite Brokered Federation of Planetary Republics and Political Bodies*.

After deciding, Teodor took his food tray and found a table just right for two humans to sit at. It was near a ceiling hung entertainment screen that was showing what looked like a high-culture video—some form of interpretive dance. Or maybe it was a martial arts demonstration. Teodor couldn't figure it out. But, then again, he really didn't care either way, he just missed being with Thresher. The dance/fight stopped and the public service videos began.

The first video showed a squadron of Fleet [fighter craft] streaking though space above a blue green planet. The announcer spoke, {"Good pay, university education, exotic ports of call. There are many good reasons to join the Fleet."} The [fighters] had entered the planet's atmosphere and were now performing rather exciting low altitude maneuvers. Around bare rocky outcrops, then, sending up clouds of snow as they raced over mountain glaciers. Now, through a forest of towering trees—with the wings of the [fighters] nearly touching the branches! The sound of their engines almost shook Teodor's lunch off the table. Then all was silence. The craft were flying low and casting their shadows over lush farmland. A little lanarkite child, surrounded by adults peacefully working the fields, looked up and waved at the passing pilots. The announcer continued, {"These are the best reasons to join. Service in the Fleet of the Realm. . . .

Meanwhile, on *Palagon Station*

We do it . . . *for them!*}"

The next video was very like one Teodor had seen before, not here in the Realm, but in a history class back at school on Earth. A pretty young cerargyrite female was holding an infant very close to her chest as she fearfully walked down a dark street in a seedy part of town. It was raining and the wet road reflected the outline of grotesque nightmare creatures lurking in the shadows. The music grew more and more ominous as the monsters closed in on their helpless victims. Then the music reached a triumphant crescendo, as a tall, handsome, young, cerargyrite male in a Guard uniform stepped out in front of the villains. He illuminated the creatures with a spotlight, drew his sidearm, and stood between the terrified mother and child and the foul enemies of the State. Of course, the huge and frighteningly deformed, but totally unarmed, bog monsters ran back into the darkness to hide. Finally, an announcer spoke, {"Strength! Honor! Loyalty! With these virtues we defend. The Guard!"} The videos ended and were then replaced by emotionally stirring instrumental music and a long duration (and Teodor thought—very worshipful) close-up of the Imperial Majesty and the statement: {"The Office of the Imperial Majesty authorized these videos."}

Teodor almost resisted the urge to say "Well, Duh!"

He brought his now empty tray to the trash receptacles and saw a human female that, just for a moment, he mistook for his mate. "No, it's not Thresher. I hope she's having a pleasant time at her interview for a change. Well, I guess I still have plenty of time for a little something else to eat. Maybe a piece of some kind of berry pastry. Oh, would I love some Earth coffee and a slice of cherry pie right now!" he thought, feeling very sad and lonely.

Thresher had worked very hard recently. *Admiral I Taisto Station* had been nearly overloaded during the pilgrimage and the Mirjami Medical Clinic was swamped. After a few days, with trash piling up and supplies needing to be unpacked, Teodor had gotten a job as well. With so many minor injuries, and some not so minor, being treated every day, it was not the most pleasant work environment he could think of, but it had been great working alongside Thresher.

Before she had started her job at the clinic, they did have a chance to visit with Heikki and Seija down at their home on Anker. Frida had come along and Teodor hadn't really minded so much. He was beginning to like the ettringite. Maybe just a little. Though he would never let her know it.

Thresher really needed that visit with her mother's old friend. They cried a little and laughed a great deal more. Teodor thought it did her a lot of good. Also, he thought, "Well, not to get mercenary about it, but it couldn't hurt getting in good with the parents of a Realm military hero."

Then it was all over, and they needed to leave so Thresher could again look for work. The Clinic management gave both Thresher and Teodor glowing recommendations and one of the long-time staff, a halotrichite named Teed, gave Thresher some information on an opening for a med tech at a university preparatory school on *Palagon Station*. Teodor uncharacteristically reasoned optimistically, "Roopertti had been the answer to Seija's prayers. Maybe, the Cerdic-Chaidam Academy would be the answer to Thresher's."

Teodor finished his dessert and thought he would shop around for something nice for his mate. Now that the lunch crowd was returning to their [afternoon] activities, the shopping area should be emptying out a little. Strangely, it wasn't. There seemed to be quite a few uniformed Citizens hurrying to take positions around the area as well. Now that he thought of it, Teodor noticed the public address announcements seemed excessive and most of them seemed to be requests for certain Citizens to go to one place or another. "Of course," Teodor thought, "somebody big must be making a token appearance to keep the mob contented. A little [bread and circuses] trick, complements of the 'Realm Ministry of Public Enlightenment."

Teodor felt he could ignore the propaganda crap and just go about his business. He noticed that across the way was a little gift shop displaying a beautiful selection of reasonably priced flowers and plants. He walked over and investigated the local equivalent of long stem roses. Only these 'roses' were bright blue, glowed in the dark for several hours (after you let them warm-up to room temperature,) and smelled all the worlds like peaches. The clerk assured him that they caused no unpleasant reaction in humans, so Teodor bought Thresher a bundle of nine and set out down what he was certain was a shortcut service passage back to where he was to meet up with her.

He had only gone a few dozen meters down the passage, when two cerargyrites blocked his way. They had that certain look that only young males of any species can develop. He wisely resisted the urge to ask them what they were rebelling against, but it didn't matter. One of them knocked the flowers from out of his hands and then stood there staring at him—like he was inviting Teodor to join in the altercation. Teodor was at a loss as to what to do. Getting assaulted was a new experience for him.

He looked around for some form of assistance and finding none, he thought he might actually have to physically defend himself. Then he remembered what Thresher had told him about growing up in the Realm. "We're never alone." she had said and told him why.

"That's it!" he thought, "Now, what would work quicker? Fire! Hull Breach! Or Kill The Imperial Majesty!" The youths didn't look too bright, so he decided to buy time. "Hey, I'm glad I ran into you two. I represent a ... well, let's just say a private little group and we're looking for a few bright young ASSASSINS to do a little job for us. That's if you have experience in that sort of thing. You aren't the two that tried to KILL THE IMPERIAL MAJESTY a year or so ago, are you? Probably not, you look smarter then that. I remember thinking it was very foolish for those two to paint, 'DEATH TO THE REALM' all over the station. Well, if you're looking to [make good money,] then it's good we ran into each other. What do you say? Can I buy you Citizens a drink and then we can talk it over? My favorite is called a HULL BREACH, but hey, FIRE is FIRE. Whatever you want is good with me. I think there's a good out-of-the-way place where we can talk privately ... just back down here." He turned slowly and started confidently walking back into the public area. All the while, trying to look unconcerned and dominating.

It didn't work out as he had planed. As Teodor moved up the walkway, he caught, out of the corner of his eye, one of the cerargyrite [punks] pull something that looked like a weapon out of his belt. Teodor picked up the pace and thought he was putting a lot of distance between himself and his would be attackers.

He was intently concentrating on himself and the two cerargyrites, but, in the back of his mind, he just thought he might be hearing alarms sounding. Suddenly, there were strange feelings in his legs, "like trying to walk down the corridor of a moving train," Teodor thought. He felt dizzy and nauseated and then something hit the back of his head like a rock and he went face down on the deck. Moments later, it all went black for him.

Had his mate been with him and not [locked-down] inside the school, she could have explained what the various alarms he heard were indicating. In chronological order the following emergency alarms occurred:

- First, "Station personnel brace for possible emergency."
- Second, the station went to [Military Action Stations!]
- Third, "Prepare for impact! Possible hull penetration!"
- And, after the station was effected by radiation from a detonated mining torpedo, "Decompression Emergency!"

The End Of
A Kripslod in the Realm

Being the First Part Of
The Kripslod's Tale

Translators' Endnotes:

Translators' Endnotes

[1] Realmspeak does not have upper and lower case letters. Instead, it has a symbol that is placed over the first letter of a sentence and another symbol that is placed over the first letter of proper nouns, some articles, and titles.

In Realmspeak the following nouns and their derivatives are always indicated (capitalized):
- Citizen (Citizens, Citizenry)
- Realm (Realmwide, Realmcare, Realmtender [money])
- Guard (when referring to the Imperial Life Guard)
- Fleet (the Realm's space navy)
- Judiciary (Judge, Judicial)
- Legislature (the law making body)
- Imperial (Empress, Emperor)
- State (Realm's government or member planetary governments)
- Lady, Sir (used as granted and hereditary titles only)
- The titles, articles and pronouns of *The One*. The deity worshiped by the State religion, *The Worship of The One*.
- References to and the names of the various gods and goddesses recognized by devotees of the *Holy Arts*. A polytheistic religion practiced by many ettringites Realmwide and by a few humans living in the Idocrase System.
- We ask your forbearance when we inadvertently fail to be consistent in carrying over these customs from Realmspeak into English. We have at times been at odds with our various editors (both human and machine) and have not always won out.

[2] In an attempt to make the reading of this book easier for our Earth-born readers, we have substituted many Realmspeak proper names instead of transliterating them. Realm and Clinohumite humans have been assigned surnames found in historical documents of the European Low Countries from the Renaissance period. Their given names are mostly taken from modern Dutch.
- We can't remember how we came to use the name, 'Thresher,' but after we did, it just kind of stuck with us.
- Except for historical references, all names in *The Kripslod's Tale* are fictitious, and so, *no* names used should be understood to have any reference to those possessing similar names on Earth.

[3] Realmspeak is the *lingua franca* (generally held to be a creole based on *Kaedyminium*) of *The Thenardite Brokered Federation of Planetary Republics and Political Bodies*. (a.k.a. the Realm) Realmspeak is itself the basis for the language used by the human inhabitants of the Republic of the Clinohumite Free People.
- Unlike most pidgin and creole types of languages, Realmspeak contains many compound nouns and syllabic abbreviations.
- In most cases, the terms used as department names by the Realm government have only one indicated (capital) letter (e.g. Realmcare. The Realmwide socialized health care system)
- Realm based private enterprises usually use two or more indicated letters if their name is compound or syllabic (e.g. RealmRock. The large mining and chemical company.)

[4] "Imperial Majesty" is a very loose translation of the Realmspeak term used for the Chief of State and head of the federal government of *The Thenardite Brokered Federation of Planetary Republics and Political Bodies* (a.k.a. the Realm.) A more accurate translation might be, "Hereditary President for Life," but as the term *president* is used for several other nation's chief executives in *The Kripslod's Tale* we thought its use in this context might cause confusion for our readers.
- During the time covered by this book, the Imperial Majesty of the Realm is the Empress Caesellia (born 1611 fTF and started her reign in 1722 fTF.) She is the daughter of Emperor Avillius (born 1563 fTF, died 1747 fTF. Reigned from 1604 fTF to 1722 fTF retired.)

[5] The SCV (system control vessel) is the largest type of warship in the Realm's arsenal. It can be thought of as a combination of portable support center, battleship, and aircraft carrier. They were originally developed as a platform for establishing and maintaining military control over a foreign planetary system. As such, they — in the days of the Empire of the Palagonites — were commonly the flagship of a military governor. In modern times they have taken on the role of being the command, support, and primary long-range offensive/defensive ship for a battle group under the command of a rear admiral.

Translators' Endnotes

[6] TFSS (Thenardite Federation Space Ship) designates a Realm Fleet warship. IGSS (Imperial Guard Space Ship) designates a Realm Military Guard warship.

[7] (See also note # 2 above) Members of the palagonite race have been assigned Roman (Latin) names.

[8] Words and sounds initiated by, or transmitted by machines will be inserted between { } brackets. This would include: computer interfaces, public address systems, warning alarms, videos and various audio playback devices.

[9] (See also note # 2 above) The names of the planets, other locations, and that of the member races themselves, have been taken from English geology and mineralogy names. There was no conscious attempt to impart any hidden meaning when assigning these names, other than in some instances to convey the texture of the original Realmspeak name.

[10] (See also note # 2 above) Members of the cerargyrite race have been assigned Finnish names.

[11] We have, rather haphazardly, included some Realmspeak words that could easily be transliterated using English letters. We felt that these words will give the narrative an authentic flavor.

[12] See also note # 2 above) Members of the ettringite race have been assigned German and Nordic names. (It seemed appropriate because they look like Doberman pinschers.)

[13] This name is a transliteration of the original Realmspeak name. We have yet to find out the species of this individual.

[14] The words, 'Fleet' and 'Guard' are integral parts of their respective compound nouns and so we will always include them in Realm military ranks (e.g. Guard Captain Adal, Fleet First Lieutenant Smith, Fleet Wing Commander HRH Princess Isolda)
- Also, HRH (his/her royal highness) is, by Realm law and custom, always included when addressing an ettringite royal.

[15] Standard units of time measurement in the Realm and the Clinohumite Republic are based on the ancient Palagonite Imperial System. At the present time, the planet Palagon makes one full orbit around its star (Proculus) in 379.65 days. This is standardized as a 380 day year with twentieth year corrections. A day is divided into 25 hours (equal to about 26.3 Earth hours) and starts at, a now arbitrary, local time considered daybreak. An hour in divided into 80 minutes and a minute is divided into 80 seconds. A year is divided into ten, 38 day months.

- The Earth term *week* has no analogous term in Realmspeak. A common work day is divided as follows:
  - First shift/watch: 'dawn' (00:01) through to 06:20
  - Second shift/watch: 06:21 through to 12:40
  - Third shift/watch: 12:41 through to 18:60
  - Fourth shift/watch: 18:61 through to 00:00
- On ships and stations the common area lights are dimmed between 12:41 and 24:79 [See also Figure #1]

For a worker in a skilled field such as medical sciences, an average work schedule would be a selection of non-consecutive shifts in three to four work days followed by two to three full days off from work. By Realm law, no Citizen is allowed to perform paid work for more than 12 ½ consecutive hours except under extreme emergency and that is still open to close State scrutiny. In addition to unpaid days off from work, most Citizens receive twenty-six to forty-eight paid vacation/personal days per year. [The Realm takes pride in near zero unemployment.]

- To align Earth to Realm chronology, a convenient date is the year of the founding of the Realm (1 fTF) which corresponds to a date in the second half of the year 1 BCE on Earth. (But keep in mind that the duration of time between 1 January of 1 BCE and 1 January of 1 CE is only one year.) One Realm year equals about 1.14 Earth years.

- Dates prior to the founding of the Realm, but after the founding of *The Empire of the Palagonites and the Peoples of the Galaxy*, are designated by the term, 'yIC.'

- The term, '*fC*' is used to designate years prior to 1 yIC (starting at 1 fC and working backwards to the beginning of time.)

[16] Sire: In earlier editions of this English translation we used the term, 'Lord' to translate the Clinohumite specific Realmspeak title found here in the Realmspeak text. In order to avoid confusion between ettringite nobles and distinguished Clinohumite (human) individuals, and to give some indications of the distinct archaic flavour of the Clinohumite dialect we have substituted the words, 'Sire' and 'Dame.' -English Translators.

[17] *Crrign* language: ag-brocht (ăg-brăhhhkt.) Ettringite alcoholic beverage. Main ingredients consist of alcohol (50-65%) fermented from potato-like starchy tubers and flavored with caramelized sugar, milk from various domesticated animals, tree resin, and a meat bouillon (stock-cube) product called, '*ag*.' Some formulations may be psychotropic or generally toxic to humans and other species. '*Brocht*' is the *Crrign* word for meat and animal product based alcoholic beverages in general.

[18] The translators have been at odds as to how this term should be shown in this text. Although, it appears as a harmless description of the individual's fur colors (outside of the context) it is (in the context) intended as a racial slur. For now, we will show this translated term as, Black and Tans. This should alert our readers to the fact that it is intended as a derogatory proper noun.

[19] *The Thenardite Brokered Federation of Planetary Republics and Political Bodies* (a.k.a. the Realm.) Sometimes referred to as The Second Realm by historians, to differentiate it from *The Empire of The Palagonites and Peoples of the Galaxy* (The First Realm.)
 • It was proclaimed in 1 fTF and the Articles of Federation were ratified by all of the original eleven States by 52 fTF.
 • A form of federal constitutional republic (tripartite) with a hereditary president (Imperial Majesty) and bicameral Legislature.
 • Upper house (House of the Planets,) consists of delegates of the member States—selected by custom of State governments.
 • Lower house (House of the Citizenry,) apportioned to States by population and chosen by direct election (universal suffrage.)
 • Senior Judiciary appointed by executive branch and ratified by both houses of the Legislature.
 • The legal system of the Realm is inquisitorial/non-adversarial

and based wholly on civil (codified) law.
- The Imperial Majesty appoints (with Legislative approval) the Judges of the Realm's High Court of the Judiciary [supreme court] and the other senior courts. The Judges of the senior courts appoint (with Executive approval) all other federal judges and their assorted staff.
- The basic set of regulations establishing civil law and orderly government in the Realm is called, the Articles of Federation (a.k.a. The Constitution of the Realm.) Printed out, the Articles of Federation would be about the size of a thirty volume English language encyclopedia.
- Additionally, the Protocols (eight in number) list the rights and obligations of the Citizenry, the member States, the various parts of government, and the thenardite species in particular.

[20] The Guard. (a.k.a. The Imperial Life Guard [archaic.]) The Guard is composed of four departments that work in close coöperation with one another. Equipment and personnel are easily and often transferred from one department to another department. Constitutionally under the control of the Judiciary and managed by the Executive (Imperial Majesty.) The departments are:
- The Federal Police (provides security and law enforcement in areas under federal control. This would include: federally operated stations, federal prisons, relocation/interment centers, military installations, federal courthouses and territories of the Realm. Also assigned as security on Fleet/Guard warships, stations and facilities under the direction of the Political Officer (a member of the Political Police assigned to maintain political orthodoxy.)
- The Military Guard (interplanetary military body similar to, but only ten percent as large as the Fleet. Responsible for enforcing smuggling and commerce laws in inter-system space. Provides the military might needed to back-up the other Guard departments in the performance of their duties. May be used to enforce federal law in member States that refuse to do so themselves.
- Political Police (provides security at political events and enforces federal voting laws. Freely empowered to investigate and to take legal action against political, commercial, and religious

[Continued on next page]

organizations for possible radical or subversive leanings. May only investigate individual Citizens (in non-public settings) with special permission from the Judiciary.

- Security Police (a Realm-wide investigative police force. Also provides security for all entitled members of Legislative, Judicial and Executive branches including the Imperial Majesty's family. 'Department Six' is the name of the Imperial Majesty's personal bodyguard.

[21] The Fleet (The primary defensive/offensive military service of the Realm. It consists of both planetary operating and space forces and is responsible for the protection of all member planets and political bodies from hostile outside forces. It can also provide emergency services when requested to do so by the government of a member State. It is constitutionally under the control of the Legislature and managed by a department of the Executive Branch called the Fleet Committee.

[22] Three asterisks in a row (* * *) are used at the end of a section of text in this English translation to indicate a passage of time.

[23] *The Republic of the Clinohumite Free People.* A self-governing (sovereign) State, founded (c 5 fTF.) by human refugees of the Ettringite Genocidal War. It allows Citizenship only to humans and is isolationist and xenophobic in foreign policy. The whole if its territory comprises just one stellar system (Alabanda) on the edge of the Realm's Third Octant. Since its 'belligerent attitude' towards the Realm led to its being subject to technological and industrial sanctions (769 fTF,) it is now believed to support itself to a large extent by controlling most of the piratical activity in and around the Realm. It is a form of timocratic republic, with a Supreme Council elected by the ship and land owning classes.

[24] In the interest of privacy, all the names of Earth-born humans in *The Kripslod's Tale* have been changed. The names used are intended to be fictitious and should not be understood to represent anyone living or dead with the same or similar name.

[25] As we have found that Mr. Kenny can't be bothered to leave the golf course long enough to come into the office to verify his hastily communicated instructions, we have had to, at times, take matters into our own hands. That being said, we have decided that the appearance of a diphthong where one was not intended will be prevented by the rather vintage use of a diaeresis mark. (e.g. naïve, coördinator, Creätor)

[26] This would have been the old route 17, not the modern limited-access interstate highway of today (2008 CE.)

[27] As best as we understand it [not much,] spaceships use a 'graviton drive' to achieve faster-than-light speeds. Apparently, there is also some kind of faster-than-light communication available. Other examples of advanced technology found in *The Kripslod's Tale* include, *apotrepein* emitters (force fields?) to protect ships, anti-matter containing anti-ship torpedoes, particle beam weapons and 'artificial' gravity on interplanetary ships (planet orbiting stations seem to use centrifugal force and not 'produced gravitons' to achieve planet-normal conditions.)

[28] "Non-Complainers." Clinohumite Space Navy slang. It has shades of meanings—from crewless drones to a term similar to the English, 'cannon fodder.' Our original working title for this chapter was taken from something Teodor said in another volume of *The Kripslod's Tale:* "Only those that prove themselves worthy get to carry a spear in the third act!"

[29] The homeworld of the ettringites (Ettring) is populated by a single race (ettringites) with a single planet-wide culture and language (*Crrign,*) governed by a single national entity, *The Holy Kingdom of the Ettringite People*—an absolute theocratic monarchy which submitted first to the Palagonite Empire and later (willingly?) joined the Realm. King Leudoberct XIV ratified the Articles of Federation making Ettring the sixth member planet in 27 fTF. Although, the federal law of the Realm gives all Citizens additional rights, the laws, society, and government of Ettring are wholly controlled by the King (considered a deity.)

[30] Ettringites have a very good sense of smell and additionally have a scent gland at the back of their necks. Without consideration to gender or social class, they always greet one another by bending forward and sniffing each other's scent glands. Ettringites never sniff members of the human race—who some (perhaps many) ettringites consider to be unholy and unnatural abominations.

[31] The Goddess Adalheidis is the goddess and personification of the star the planet Ettring orbits (Adalheid.) It is said that she mated with the God Archembald (god of rain/water) and gave birth to the planet Ettring, who in turn gave birth to the ettringite race (without the need for a mate.) She is also believed to be responsible for protecting Ettring from cosmic danger and disturbance. Interestingly, despite her worthy duties and accomplishments, her worship has fallen behind that of the more 'popular' gods and goddesses in recent times.

[32] Taciturnians and their *Cult of Adalheidis:* A secret society modeled after the ancient mystery religion of the same name. The High Priest of Adalheidis is looked on as the final authority in all matters pertaining to the worship of the goddess Adalheidis, but the leaders of the cult are thought to act independently in most cases. Founded as a racist social organization by ettringite Fleet officers sometime after 1690 fTF. Not officially sanctioned by the Religious Office of the King of the Ettringites.

[33] For the most part we have transliterated halotrichite names.

[34] The Realmspeak word used here could be better translated by the Yiddish word, *'Chutzpah.'* as it indicates a level of brazenness bordering on mental illness.

[35] Or, 'extraordinary.'

[36] The mining station on the asteroid Iconium was rebuilt, to a large extent, with funding provided by the archaeologist and religious instructor, Professor Hubrecht Gherstecore. He also added the Latin language word, *'Phoenix'* to the station's name.

[37] In Realm nomenclature, and by extension most civilizations using Realmspeak (like the Clinohumites), moons are named by adding their orbit number to the planet's name (numbered closest in to outermost). For example: Breithaupt-Seven is the seventh moon orbiting the planet Breithaupt. Some moons may also also have a traditional (pre-spaceflight) common name.

[38] The primary asteroid belt(s) found in the Alabanda System (of which Clinohum is the third planet) is unlike the Main Belt found in the Solar System. Alabanda's belt is much more recently formed (less then 10,000 Earth years) and far more densely populated with both large and small asteroid bodies. It is also comprised of two separate fields—intersecting, but orbiting on very different planes. Belt α orbits on the same plane as the six planets in the system and belt β orbit is tilted at 67 degrees. It is believed (by some) to be the result of a rocky planet being intentionally destroyed some five thousand (Palagon) years ago. Perhaps by the same civilization that left artifacts on planets and moons throughout the system.

If this theory is true and if the original planet was situated in the same orbit as belt α, then the first four original planets were rocky, the fifth was a gas giant, the sixth (now broken up) was rocky and the seventh was a gas giant almost large enough to be considered a failed star.

[39] In the English translation, we will use *italics* to indicate:
- Names of art and literary works.
- Names of publications.
- Names of ships.
- Names of space stations (including the word *station*, if used.)
- Full names of religious and political organizations.
- Non-English words retained or inserted into the translation.

[40] Realmspeak: Kripslod (*Krĭps·lŏd,*) a tool of inferior design that causes injury to the user or to sensitive equipment. For an Earth example consider a drilling hammer made from white cast iron. The term is often used in Realmspeak where, 'jerk,' or 'idiot' would be used in English.

[41] The Sthene system is the Realm's closest stellar system, with a permanent settlement, to the boarder with the Clinohumite Republic. It lies at the outer edge of the Third Octant [military district] and is the home of the lightly inhabited [Earth-like] planet Digenite. Located within the system are several military and civilian complexes including: a Realmcustoms facility located on the fourteenth moon of a small gas giant, a Fleet Support Facility, and a commercial shipping and distribution hub called *Digenite Station*. The Sthene system is also a home port for one of the two SCV Battlegroups assigned to Fleet Operations Third Octant.

[42] The original Realmspeak word used here was the syllabic abbreviation, '*Chasmird*.' It is taken from the Realmspeak term, '*Chasjeph*' (specialist in) + '*Mirdruith*' (medical sciences)

[43] This is the actual term used in the Realmspeak manuscript. A footnote in that text explains the word as follows: "From the Earth human language, German. It means, 'a person one has familial affection for' + 'little or small.' The usual context is that of a Citizen referencing their mate in an playful way."

[44] This is probably intended to set the mood, as it is technically incorrect. In the Realm, all Citizens are entitled to the basic necessities of life, including food and shelter. If a Citizen is unable to supply their own needs the the Office of the Imperial Majesty will proved them. Those found to be chronic malingers can be relocated to a place more convenient for the State, but perhaps less pleasant to the recipient of the aid.

[45] Modern English term for love story. The Realmspeak word used here means, 'inspiring [legal] mating thoughts.' There is a different word in Realmspeak for subjects similar to the English, 'pornography.'

[46] Literally: 'Access Cover + lectures.' From the custom of Fleet chief crewpersons standing on raised covers to service chases and races. This would give them a more prominent place to lecture their subordinates from.

[47]   Literally: 'Purging.' Meaning, purging atmospheric gas supply lines to remove contaminants. Used here to denote a Citizen loudly and tediously expressing stupid opinions to others.

[48]   To remove any confusion, we thought it best to explain that at this point in the text, the narrator takes us back eight months and through the rest of this volume we move ahead chronologically until we begin chapter Twenty-Three at this very point in time.

[49]   Non-recreational common areas on a station along which merchants set up shops. May also include food vending areas.

[50]   See also note # 2 above) We have transliterated the names of members of the halotrichite race.

[51]   RSDS: '<u>R</u>ealm' + '<u>S</u>pacer' (meaning, 'interstellar') + <u>D</u>elivery <u>S</u>ervice. A prominent inter-Realm freight delivery company.

[52]   Literally: 'Honor Day for Realm Mothers.'

[53]   Several humans have expressed this opinion in other books of *The Kripslod's Tale*. Perhaps we have grown accustomed to them, but whatever the reason, the English translators do not find the printed illustrations of thenardites in their bipedal configuration to be any more unpleasant to look at than the other races shown. They do have a 'Hollywood werewolf' look about them, more so then the other canine-like race, the ettringites do.
• Also, we have not seen any illustrations of a bipedal thenardite in a uniform and so we do not know how it is possible for someone to recognize that they are in uniform and yet see their stripes at the same time.

Translators' Endnotes

[54] We have had questions about this comment that Thresher makes here (From very attentive readers, no doubt.) They have wondered why a daughter of a Fleet chief crewperson would fail to recognize this rank insignia, given that the number of 'icons' denoting ranks follow a logical progression. Who knows, maybe it is just 'poetic license.' We will be adding a color chart of Fleet and Guard rank insignia to some future additions of this translation, so that you can judge for yourself.

[55] The Realmspeak term we translated as 'smile' is a species-neutral term denoting a gesture of pleasantness or friendliness. It does not in all species indicate the use of facial movement. Specifically with reference to halotrichites it involves arm and hand gestures as well as gestures with the eyes and mouth. Since ettringites are spoken of as closely resembling Earth dogs, we feel that it is possible that the Guard Admiral gave what could be called a 'happy dog' smile. We find a reference to that look when a thenardite is spoken of by a human in another Realmspeak text.

[56] Among humans living in the Realm it is common, but in no way universal, for one member (regardless of gender) of the legally mated pairing to substitute their mate's family name in place of their own (about 20% of the time, on average.) The pair may also create a totally new family name (25%,) add the two family names together (10%,) or do nothing and just keep separate family names (45%.) We have not yet seen any studies involving other species that commonly use both a given and a family name.

[57] A short and possibly somewhat inaccurate time line for Thresher Selverlinck, that we patched together from this and other books, is as follows:
- Born on a Fleet support station in 1718 fTF (1959-1960 CE)
- Mother (Sanne Selverlinck) died on TFSS *Skyfish* in 1723 fTF
- Started university in 1738 fTF (?)
- Graduated as a med tech in 1742 fTF
- Met Teodor Korzeniowski on *Anatase* (RSDS) *Station*, 1756 fTF

[58] Ettringite names: In common practice an ettringite has only one name, their individual scent giving non-verbal proof of the identities of their parents as well as to the larger [tribal] unit to which they are related. In verbal or printed references an ettringite might be referred to by patronymic or matronymic means, such as, Frida the daughter of Evert (if Evert has been previously introduced or is well known.) Other excepted ways would include: Frida the daughter of Klara, Frida the paternal granddaughter of Poldi, Frida of the [tribe] of Raimund (from the common ancestor of all those who are known to possess the same [tribal] scent. Other forms are also possible.

- In official record keeping of the Realm all Citizens and long-term visitors are issued a CIN or Citizen Identification Number. This CIN indicates one and only one individual from birth, through life and death and into bureaucratic *Valhalla*. Since the location of all Citizens is known or can be known at all times, the CIN can also be used as an address. (Like a postal address, a State issued identification card and a social welfare card all in one.)

- The particular ettringite female spoken of here is therefore, Frida the daughter of Evert (and Klara) who smells like a member of the Raimunds, CIN005176540017332974930274940. Broken down that number consists of: CIN 005 (ettringite) + 17654 (born on the planet Alunite) + 001733 (in the year (fTF only, pre-fTF is indicated by, 000000)) + 2974930274940 (unique number.)

- Just a little piece of trivia: The noted thenardite religious instructor Tymorann Alphrontex's number is: CIN000000000000000000000000000.

[59] Fortesgrr (fōr·tĕs·g[ĕ]rrr) is hot beverage consumed primarily by ettringites who find it to be a moderate stimulant. Humans sometimes drink it as a strong depressant. It is highly toxic to cerargyrites and halotrichites.

[60] The German word '*Tante*' (meaning, Aunt or Auntie) was in the original Realmspeak text. As we understand it, Karen once lived on the planet Earth. In the Kingdom of Prussia (from 1862 CE,) the German Empire, the Wiemar Republic, the United States of America (c 1925-1934 CE) and Germany (until early 1939 CE.)

Translators' Endnotes

[61] Guard Admiral Reinier may be expressing a common opinion and not giving an indication as to whether ettringite erythrocytes are enucleate like Earth mammals or not.

[62] Literally: 'The offspring of money.' A hatchling produced by the aid of a [male] prostitute. A strong derogatory term.

[63] [Original Realmspeak footnote] Earth human language, German: 'Repeatedly cursed by a deity.'

[64] Sheet music for *Un bel dì, vedremo* -by Giacomo Puccini is available at UR Research (University of Rochester) (http://hdl.handle.net/1802/24437)

[65] Here is one of the few places in the original Realmspeak text where the part of creation that all physical beings exist in is actually identified as a PLACE, rather than a mathematical concept. Usually the terms used in Realmspeak would translate as: continuüm (the part of creation that can be described in four dimensions and using physical laws) and exo-continuüm (for parts of creation that do not obey 'natural' laws (i.e. Heaven, the supernatural realm, or the spirit world.)

[66] Teodor is using the 'Clinohumite' word for the highest enlisted (non-officer) rank.

[67] We substituted the original Realmspeak word which required sounds not found in English, with this name of a naturally occurring tantalum oxide.

[68] Originally (in older editions of this book) the English word, 'Sentient' (able to experience sensations) was used to translate the Realmspeak word used here. For this edition we have substituted, 'sapience' (wisdom or judgment) as we feel that, on further study, this would be a more accurate translation.

[69] Sheet music for *Treue Liebe* -by Friedrich Silcher and Helmine von Chezy is available from the IMSLP/Petrucci Music Library (www.imslp.org/wiki/Treue_Liebe(Silcher,_Friedrich))

[70] Palagonite names: The most common naming convention among palagonites (with the exception of the Imperial family) is for males: personal name + maternal grandfather's personal name + father's family name. For females: personal name + paternal grandmother's personal name + mother's family name. Actual palagonite names (in *Kaedyminium*) are extremely long. Personal names can run to twelve characters (sounds) and family names up to forty characters (sounds.) We have substituted these 'full' names with a single Latin name to identify palagonite Citizens in the text.

[71] In previous editions of this book, we had split this chapter into three parts: Chapter 18 *Admiral I Taisto Station*, Chapter 19 *The Princess Agrippina Room*, and Chapter 21 *Gainful Employment*.

[72] Here is an example of the need to substitute what Teodor really said for something that will not violate copyright law. We made this replacement reference up. We wouldn't need to make stuff up if Mr. Kenny would just put the putter down long enough to secure permission for us to use Teodor's actual Earth references.
(The actual reference was from a screenplay by Rod Serling and based on a story by Damon Knight.)

[73] Some Earth animals have analogous representatives in the Realm and therefore Teodor's ideas are easily translated between English and Realmspeak. In this case, the original Realmspeak text had to have a lengthy footnote explaining what Teodor was thinking about.

[74] We think that this reference is vague enough to safely leave unchanged without fear of violating copyright here on Earth. -English translators.

[75] Literally: 'Attitude of a Fleet Second Ensign.' Just out of Fleet School (with the lowest passing grades possible) and so full of oneself. A terror to Fleet crewpersons the Realm over.

[76] We used a little creative license in order to give an impression of how Frida's translated (or as Teodor would say. "store-bought") English would have sounded.
* If the surveillance systems had understood Frida's use of a racial slur in a public place, she would have faced a civilian fine and because she was in uniform also a Guard reprimand. What Teodor said would probably have required further scrutiny to decipher.

[77] An egg-laying mammal, native to Ettring, and now raised Realmwide for its meat. They are small (10-15 Kg) with dark brown fur. Several of its internal organs are considered delicacies by ettringites. Besides being used for food, the *rafn* is sometimes allowed to forage around less well-tended stations and ships in order to keep the number of invasive invertebrate creatures in check.

[78] Realmspeak slang for a carnivore or omnivore that lives as a herbivore by choice.

[79] A small, but quickly growing sect (off shoot) of the Realm State religion. Adherents claim that their religion is not a sect, but in point of fact the original and true religion practiced by the thenardites since creation. Groups can be found in almost every population center in the Realm and in neighboring nations. The official publication is called, *The Journal of the Way of The One*.

[80] Literally, 'Cropper,' meaning an ettringite with cropped ears. Legally only members of the Royal Family of the ettringites, offspring of croppers with hereditary privileges, and those appointed by the reigning monarch of the ettringites are permitted to have cropped ears. This rule applies even for actors depicting croppers. In the Realm, ettringite croppers are legally entitled to be called, 'Sir' or 'Lady,' unless they already have the right to a higher title such as, 'HRH' (His/Her Royal Highness)

[81] Ofimdocs (Office of the Imperial Majesty, Department of Citizen Support.) [we suggest you pronounce it: Ăwf▪ Ĭm▪ Dŏcs]

[82] [Original Realmspeak footnote] A racial slur.
- English Translators note: The bonobo is a sub-species of the Earth primate genus *Pan*, "Chimpanzee." (*Pan paniscus*)

[83] In Realmspeak, pronouns, personal pronouns and titles referring to The One are always indicated (capitalized.)
- The thenardites refer to their God as genderless, 'It.'
- It seems that most other races use the masculine, 'He.'

[84] Meaning: Fourth in importance. Used in both the Fleet and the Guard to refer to housekeeping assignments or KP (kitchen police) duties.

[85] Members of the State religion, *The Worship of The One* (officially, all Citizens who have not registered their membership in another State recognized faith) would call themselves, 'Worshipers of The One.' Members of, *The Way of The One* call themselves, 'Adherents of The Way of The One (never Way'rs.) Members of the ettringite polytheistic religion, *The Holy Art*, as overseen by the King of the Ettringite people, call themselves, 'Fearers of the Gods.'

[86] An Ettring native herbivore. About the size and temperament of an Earth sheep. It lives wild in herds and is considered a tasty, quick and easy to acquire meal when vacationing in rural country.

[87] Of course we substituted English numbers, letters and symbols for what he would have said in the *Crrign* language.

[88] The *Crrign* term translated here is considered extremely racist and offensive in the Realm. It was used by ettringites to refer to the humans they owned in pre-civil war times.

[89] Basel Duty Officer. This is a Realm military assignment. The Basel station controls basic ship functions (life support, anti-drift, internal systems, etc.) while the ship is docked or at rest.

[End of Translators' Notes]

Coming Distractions

What's coming up in the next exciting volume of

The Kripslod's Tale?

<u>Perhaps</u> one of these stories:

- *"Leave it to the Kripslod."* Teodor is sent to a maximum security asylum for the criminally insane. There he regales his fellow inmates with stories from his childhood in Utica.

- *"A Tale of Two Kripslods."* Teodor finds he is replaced by an evil doppelgänger. Hilarity ensues.

- *"My Strudel!"* Teodor becomes the new Imperial Majesty.

- *"A Kripslod Lost! A Lady Found!"* Teodor is unable to appear in this volume due to a previous engagement. We understand he will be touring with the Terlinguaite-Five Heavy Opera Company's production of the fabulous new musical version of Anton Pavlovich Chekov's *Uncle Vanya*.
  ♬ "You had no joy in your life, but wait, but wait. We shall rest, we shall rest. Weee shaaaal reeeest Fa la la do si do."♪

- *"The Hound of the Kripslods."* An evil danger prowls the moors of Molybdenite Nineteen-Nineteen and Six "

- *"Spleen of Insufficient Light."* Guard Junior Chief Crewperson Hondenaghele Parynghoot is sent deep into the mysterious jungles of Nantokite-Twelve. His assignment? To give renegade Fleet Senior Captain Rycquaerdt Raywaerdt a little light. "The unpleasantness! The unpleasantness!"

Available wherever books are made sticky by cheap layabouts who never purchase books. They just read them in the coffee shop while they take advantage of the free WiFi.

Made in the USA
Columbia, SC
24 September 2018